*To the one who taught me to rise
above it, this is yours.*

Acknowledgements

Thank you, Professors Popovic, Giles and Tarc for your serendipitous contribution to providing the necessities for me to write this novel, I can say with certainty that I never would have been able to write were it not for your collective kindness, wisdom and support. Also, I do not believe in coincidence so I am grateful for the ordinance that brought us together.

For my mother-in-law: *Mettendo da parte il dovere, vorrei ringraziare mia suocera per aver dato con tutto il cuore. E per aver nutrito la mia famiglia con il miglior cibo del mondo consegnato alla mia porta dal cuore della nonna. Sarebbe stato impossibile senza di te. Un abbraccio forte, forte.*

I would like to thank my Aunt Sharron, for supporting me as my father would have done. I would also like to thank my sister, for drowning out my negative self-talk and for rising with me on this journey. Thank you to my son for your beautiful constant inquiry and my daughter for your genius and kind heart. Thank you to my husband, the rock on which I build this life.

Our Life in Red Jell-O

BY
Kerry Greco

TABLE OF CONTENTS

PROLOGUE

I've never told anyone this before, but I remember being born. I mean I actually remember leaving my mother's body and entering the world. I think every single human being remembers being born, but they just forget that they remember. I don't have memories of being in utero (with a John Travolta voice over dictating my thoughts) but exiting a place of absolute sustenance, a place with no concept of want or I, and being contorted by a series of malleable bone crushing spasms until you are thrust into a space of I and want, hurt like hell. For that reason, the sheer pain of the moment, I remember it. And you would too if you let yourself. Forever is in that moment just before birth, just before the pain starts. And as for how I have come to know this truth, well that's where the story comes in, the little tale of proof that the universe is not as unfathomable as Beckett might have suspected. So, let me remind you of where forever is, you will thank me in the end, but I don't even have to tell you that because you can sense it already.

P.S. Some parts of this story can be read with children. So, you can read the other parts on your own but don't have to stop reading when it comes time to put the kids to bed. I will let you know when those parts begin and end because some parts are just for us grownups. I will use this font for the parts that should NEVER, EVER, be read by kids, and *this font for the kid friendly parts.*

PROLOGUE

I've never told anyone this before, but I remember being born. I mean I actually remember leaving my mother's body and entering the world. I think every single human being remembers being born, but they just forget that they remember. I don't have memories of being in utero (with a John Travolta voice over dictating my thoughts) but exiting a place of absolute sustenance, a place with no concept of *want* or *I*, and being contorted by a series of malleable bone crushing spasms until you are thrust into a space of *I* and *want*, hurt like hell. For that reason, the sheer pain of the moment, I remember it. And you would too if you let yourself. Forever is in that moment just before birth, just before the pain starts. And as for how I have come to know this truth, well that's where the story comes in, the little tale of proof that the universe is not as unfathomable as Beckett might have suspected. So, let me remind you of where forever is, you will thank me in the end, but I don't even have to tell you that because you can sense it already.

P.S. Some parts of this story can be read with children. So, you can read the other parts on your own but don't have to stop reading when it comes time to put the kids to bed. I will let you know when those parts begin and end because some parts are just for us grownups. I will use this font for the parts that should NEVER, EVER, be read by kids, *and this font for the kid friendly parts.* Also know that some of what you are about to read is absolute truth and some is fiction, and it will surprise you to know which is which.

CHAPTER 1: THE DEVIL AND THE ANGEL

Half hazed and euphoric from the anaesthesia, Frances came to her senses just after she managed to embarrass herself by pledging her love to the doctors and attendants who were wheeling her from surgery into the recovery room. A strange thing happened just as she said it; the four medical professionals did the only thing they could to restore dignity to the doped-up patient; they turned their backs on her and faced the wall, and it worked. The surgery had been a success. Apart from the fact that she lost her daughter just as she entered the second trimester, the haemorrhage had been cauterised and so she was free to begin healing. Just before she lost consciousness, on exactly the 11th hour, of the 11th day of the 11th month, in the deafening silence of the busy ER, she passed a large clot in the washroom, and from then on Remembrance Day called to mind the disposal of the baby in the garbage bin. Alban was waiting for her when she came to her senses in the recovery room, and they laughed a little at the embarrassment of her unabashed expression of love to a group of strangers during the hallway incident with the doctors. The chuckle cut through sadness of the loss of their baby and for a moment they felt grateful that at least they still had each other.

He whisked her off to an all-inclusive vacation that Christmas and they enjoyed New Year's Eve on the beach with some fireworks and a stray dog before going back to the reality of making a baby. Alban told Frances that he loved her on their first date, and although this should have made her skeptical, it didn't for some reason. They met at a Halloween party at Squirley's on Queen West, and, as God is my witness, he was dressed as a devil, and she an angel.

It wasn't long after the miscarriage that Frances was pregnant again, at least for a week anyway, something the doctor referred to as a false positive, but after four of them in a row, she began referring to them as positively false, (in a voice that suggested they keep calm and carry on) when she would break the news to Alban. After that she managed to get into her fifth week only to awake with blinding pain in her lower left side brought on by an ectopic pregnancy. She ended up in the ER once again, with another successful surgery that saw the removal of her left fallopian tube. This time as she was wheeled to the recovery room, encumbered by anesthesia, she clutched the arm of the attendant and asked him if her baby would have survived had she not removed the tube. He did not dignify her question with a response.

Frances never did share this recovery story with Alban. This time Alban went to a breeder and brought home a puppy, part golden retriever, part poodle, and part transcendent being, and Frances decided to call her Maggie.

Maggie was a large but agile dog, and her daunting size did not match her gregarious character. For a dog, Maggie had adeptly mastered the art of human expressiveness to the point where Frances quickly learned to read her furry red face and sprang to meet her needs before Maggie even knew she had them. Sensing Maggie's thirst for example, Frances would bring her freshwater and hold her dish steady while Maggie lapped it up, or noticing Maggie turn her nose up at kibble, Frances roasted chicken and sweet potato and heap generous portions into Maggie's stainless-steel dog dish. She set the dish into the crafted wooden stand that had been ergonomically designed to avoid neck strain in tall dogs and watch Maggie eat. Even dinners out became all about which patio table was close enough for Maggie to sit beside them without actually being on the property of the restaurant so as not to infringe on any food safety regulations. Then, while they ate, Frances relished the passers-by that stopped to comment on Maggie's beauty, for few could resist Maggie's stately demeanor, because whether she was standing, sitting, or lying down, Maggie was always strikingly present.

Everyone on the block loved Maggie and often she could be found in the yards of children in the neighbourhood who had taken to calling on her for random playdates and Maggie took to heart the task of entertaining them as her purpose for being, but in truth she awaited the ruffle of her puffy lid from

Frances' loving hand and the heartfelt *Good Girl* was Maggie's reason for being, and all she ever needed to be content.

Instead of sleeping in a crate at night, like most puppies, Maggie slept at Frances's bedside in her large memory foam dog bed, settled to sleep by a preservative and grain free, all natural, peanut butter pumpkin treat, presumed by Frances to be Maggie's favourite. In lieu of the crate Frances kept a wakeful ear throughout the night to keep Maggie safe and was in tune to even the slightest of Maggie's movements. Sometimes Frances would wake because she had to pee, but she would hold it to be in solidarity with Maggie. So, while Alban and Maggie slept peacefully in their Feng Shui bedroom, Frances teetered between being awoken by her full bladder or Maggie running in her sleep. Training Maggie was easy because she behaved like a service dog from the get-go, living at Frances's heel and awaiting commands that she obediently and instantly followed. She enjoyed her treats but mostly wanted to please Frances. As Maggie grew, so too did her attachment to Frances, for the pair scarcely parted and like Mary and her little lamb, wherever Frances went Maggie was sure to go.

CHAPTER 2: RED JELL-O

As often happens Frances was so distracted with Maggie that she hadn't even noticed missing her period and it wasn't until Alban had opened a bottle of wine one evening that just prior to taking her first sip, she broke out of a haze of forethought and looking at Alban with a bit of a stunned expression she informed him that she had missed her period, which sent him on a quick errand to the pharmacy for a test that sure enough turned out to be positive.

This pregnancy was smooth in that it was carried to full term, in fact the night her water broke Frances was a week overdue, so she had indeed exceeded the expectation of expecting. They arrived at the hospital fully prepared for labour and delivery and their room mimicked a Lamaze class with an inflated birthing ball and a lower back massager sitting beside Alban on the small couch as he practiced breathing techniques in preparation for what was to come, and the sight of all this was enough to garner an approving nod from the attending obstetrician.

Twenty-three hours later Frances lay on her side feeling completely numb from the epidural she had begged for because she thought the pain was sure to kill her, staring at a monitor of the baby's vital signs while Alban sat in an adjacent chair watching the same screen with an equal measure of intent.

It had been a long night and day but neither felt fatigue as they watched the baby's heart rate dip and rise, and when a different obstetrician suggested a c-section out of concern for the fluttering of their baby's tiny heart, they both nodded imploringly to her, in silent unison they begged the doctor to save their baby. In the sterile surgical room Alban held Frances's hand and stayed as close to her face as he could, for he did not dare to risk being able to see behind the curtain that separated them from the lower half of her body. As the surgeon began the process of cutting the baby out Frances was gripped with fear, maybe terror is a better word, at the possibility of losing her baby or dying right there on the table, but you wouldn't know it from looking at her. She closed her eyes and mentally recited prayers, like she had always done when she was afraid, which gave the outward appearance of pure calm and tranquility to the anesthesiologist and Alban, the only two people who could see her. Even when they couldn't get the baby out because it was caught in a tug of war between the surgeon and her uterus, Frances stayed still and did not utter a sound at the aggressive jostling of her body. The turmoil below the curtain continued until there was a point of deep pressure, as if something was about to crack and Frances finally let out a groan beneath its weight. It was then that the shift happened, that the calm penetrated the fear for real and although Frances had yet to hear the baby cry, she felt the new being, she felt all being, she felt her own being, she felt her internal eternal.

Now feelings like this are inarticulable, but if I have to use human words, and specifically the English language to describe that which must be felt on a sentient level, here's what I would say (by the way we are about to begin a kid friendly part, and this is the beginning of the book for kids):

In order to help us understand how Frances felt in that moment let me start by taking us back to a treat you might enjoy from time to time, Jell O (and let's make it red for fun). Imagine that the earth's atmosphere and everything above and below it is made of red Jell O. Picture it, everyone, and everything you know and recognize in the world going about their respective business all the while immersed in red Jell O. But of course, this is not just regular old red Jell O, this is a special red Jell O because it is a magical force that gives life to everything. It gives us life and keeps us alive, and by us, I mean me and you, so no matter who you are, what you are, or where you are, you and I are connected because we are brought to life in and by the same red Jell O. The red Jell O has always been here, will always be here, it is unaffected by time just as some part of us is unaffected by time, and our job while we are here is to see the red Jell O in everyone and everything, we encounter without actually seeing it. So, the red of the Jell O is magic as well because it is an invisible

red.   That means to us the red Jell O is
transparent, but every time we see a bird,
a rock, a human being, or anything else
kicking around on this planet we know that
we are connected to it through the magical
red Jell O that we can't see. Now I will
get to the best part, just because we can't
see the red Jell O doesn't mean we don't
know it's there because we can feel it
(like Frances did today). Everyone in the
world can feel it if they want to. And
that's it.   We have gone as far as
knowledge can take us because the rest must
be felt, can be felt. Go on, give it a
try. Immerse yourself in the red Jell O
and see if you can feel it. Whatever it
is you are sensing cannot be described in
this story that's for certain, but it can
be felt. When you see the red Jell O in
someone you see them for who they are: the
only person in the world who has ever been,
or who will ever be created like they are,
and that describes everyone who is here
now, everyone who ever existed before, and
everyone that will ever exist in the
future. Like Easter eggs being decorated,
we are dipped into a red Jell O life force
for a bit, and come to life through it,
until we dissolve back into it. So, when
we feel the red Jell O, or clear Jell O,
or something commonly known as air, we
realize that we are vivified by the same
thing, and like that thing we are outside
time and space, so some part of us will
always be here in the form of red Jell O.
And the very very best part is that

EVERYONE has access to the red Jell O, they just have to be still enough to sense it (we will talk about that later) and it's never too late to try.

Frances felt the red Jell-O when she heard the first sound her baby ever made, which was a delicate grunt but not a cry, and then a doctor brought the baby around the curtain and they saw each other for the first time, immersed in red Jell-O, two beautiful Easter eggs, ready for the dance of life.

CHAPTER 3: THE SWORD AND THE ROCK

Contrary to what the last sentence implies, and as you might have detected from the number of pages remaining, Frances and Viola (named after Shakespeare's muse) do not live happily ever after. For struggle finds all humans, it comes, and it goes, yet it is how we witness the struggle that counts in the end. But of course, how we see something depends on our vantage point, like the large weeping willow tree that Frances admired from her front window. It was tall and lush, and Frances felt like it was a part of her for some reason. When Frances saw this tree, even when she was far from home on a long walk with Maggie and she could catch just the top of it, she knew that the tip of the tree marked her home, her place on the planet, the place for Viola to grow. Little did she know that it was that very tree that would take everything from her and bring her to the darkest place on earth.

The first few months of life with Viola held a magic that Frances had never known. As Frances acted with delicate care of her baby's every need she spent time transfixed in a state of bliss provided by the endless dark wonder of Viola's eyes. I think it is important to describe the arresting power of Viola's eyes for a moment, for like the charm of Maggie's striking presence, all who had the pleasure of seeing them couldn't help but stop whatever they were doing and stare into the ocean depth of the two little dark circles, caught in a small spell as they did so. Frances lived in this perpetual contented state, and those first few months of Viola's life brought a pure unadulterated bliss into Frances's world and everyone who had the good fortune of being around them caught a little slice of the euphoria. The neighbourhood kids clambered over to the stroller encumbered by their winter gear whenever Frances happened to be outside, all with the intent of seeing the baby and each in their own way letting out a beautiful expression of *"awwww"* or *"she's so cute"* or simply laughing with delight as only children can when they encounter the wonders of life. Sometimes they still called on Maggie to come and play in their respective yards but since Viola's first homecoming Maggie could not be coaxed away from her, and since she was always with Frances, Maggie needn't pick a favourite. So the children would lovingly dote on the baby and be on their way sans Maggie. Maggie now slept in the hallway at night, equidistant from both Frances and Viola, the ever-present defender at the ready.

If Frances heard a love song on the radio, it was about the love she felt for her daughter and even corny pop songs took on a whole new meaning when she sang a top ten to her bundle. So our little Viola continued to grow in the bliss bubble together with her mother, who oscillated between waves of joy and gratitude, until the surface tension that destroys all bubbles came for theirs. Once, late at night after nursing Viola to sleep, Frances propped the baby up on her shoulder and rocked back and forth when a single thought deflated the world they had built as it penetrated Frances' mind in the still of the night. The thought was more of a question, and it sliced Frances in two the second she heard no one in particular ask inside her head: *what if Viola is harmed in some way?* Frances responded to this thought by praying slowly and methodically for her child's safety, she rocked for a long time with Viola asleep on her shoulder, imagining a shield from harm for her baby's little body in and in great detail she mentally placed a barrier between harm and every hair on Viola's delicate head. After a long time spent conjuring protection for Viola, Frances finally grew tired and laid the baby back in her crib bidding her the sweetest of dreams. She joined Alban in bed but for the first time since her baby was born there was something not quite right, and so like the princess and the pea she drifted off to sleep, and as though she were placing a sword in a rock, she wrapped her pinkie finger in Alban's hand for comfort, knowing she would be secure with him until she decided to remove it.

I feel like now is as good a time as any to talk about Alban. Life was simple for Alban. While he watched those around him grapple with their respective choices in life: partnership, singlehood, parenthood, couple hood, political views, scholarship, travel, career and all of the sidelines that happen to those choices: illness, addictions, accidents, financial struggle, unrequited love and every other one of Murphy's laws, he simply chose Frances, and seeing her eyes shine was the litmus test for every decision he ever made from the moment he met her. In turn Frances tacitly decided that she would follow Alban through life partly because she loved and trusted him but mostly because she hated making decisions, so she borrowed a page from the book of Ruth, and as inadvertent as her actions were, she had one maxim when it came to her husband: *whither thou goest, I will go.* From what you have read so far, I think there is little surprise that Alban and Frances are a well-matched pair, but I think it is also important to tell the story of what led to their partnership. I mentioned the Halloween party at Squirly's that brought them together but what I left out is that both were otherwise engaged on the night they met, well maybe not engaged but they were dating other people.

I will spare the details of their respective exes but tell you how they ended up knowing each other when circumstances being what they were dictate that it should never have happened, and you are free to believe it or not. I will start by saying that two things had to occur in one night in order for Frances and Alban to meet. The first was a dated childhood party game and the second was a broken high heel shoe. Although Frances and Alban had never actually met before that night, they did run in the same circles and were surprised to eventually discover that they had known the same people since childhood and had probably been in the same room for various reasons several times before they met. So, on this particular Halloween night, Alban as you know is dressed as a devil and Frances an angel but allow me to elaborate on the intricate detail of the costumes. Frances wore a sheer, white, flowy number with wings, a halo, stiletto shoes and white gloves and she looked like a long-haired pixie. Alban wore a tuxedo with bell bottom pants, platform shoes, and a cape with red satin lining, he had little horns glued to his head and it was noted by many that night that his facial features perfectly aligned with the costume and, forgive the irony but that *he made a really good devil*. Alban had purchased his shoes and bell-bottomed tuxedo from a second-hand store but he splurged and bought the cape from Malabar's costume shop. The only reason he bought the platform shoes was because the bell bottom tuxedo he found was a really good fit and he had to complete the look.

He didn't foresee that one of the organizers of the event would decide that an apple bobbing station would be fun and that he would be sitting beside a barrel of water and apples, kept at exactly 102 degrees Fahrenheit. Of course no one covered in face paint (or in their right mind) would bob for apples so the barrel was eventually placed on the floor out of the way but it was left plugged in and a stream of steam flowed directly to Alban's left platform heel softening the old glue, so that when he stood up all it took for the heel to be severed from the shoe was the quick clack of his first step. This wouldn't have been so bad if the group he was with hadn't just decided to leave Squirly's for another party, which meant that Alban found himself in the position of either hobbling around all night or going back to his apartment to change his shoes, and he of course picked the latter option. His girlfriend at the time was three sheets to the wind and headed to the other party with the promise of catching up with him later.

Frances was with her best friend that night because her boyfriend (who was a miserable sort of person to whom she was always apologizing for some reason or another) told her that he was staying home that night, when in actuality he went somewhere else and was at that very moment engaged in a flirty conversation with another woman. So as Alban hobbled towards the exit, he bumped into Frances' best friend who upon seeing he was dressed as a disco devil, in a volume that had been raised by the rye and ginger she consumed, squealed with delight about how he had to meet her best friend, took his hand, and dragged him to the booth they were occupying. That was when Alban saw Frances for the first time, the unassuming angel, taking a sip of her corona with lime and at that moment he forgot all about the excuse he was coming up with to make his hasty getaway, and he sat down at the table.

They sipped and chatted and near the end of the night talked about future plans and Alban mentioned that he and his girlfriend didn't want kids at which point Frances' best friend, whose name is Ann Maria Grover, but whom Frances always called Grover, enthusiastically agreed, and talked for a long time about a cousin she had that never wanted kids but had them anyway and the debacle that ensued in the life of her cousin's family as a result. She then admitted that she herself was not inclined to make babies and that whoever she ended up with should be content with dogs. Frances agreed sincerely with Grover on this point, for they had been friends since childhood and she knew Grover had never wanted to be a parent, but she added incredulously that for herself there was nothing else on earth she wanted more than motherhood, and the clouds seemed to part for Alban and as she said it, for he looked into her eyes and realised he had been wrong all along about not wanting children, and that indeed there was nothing else to be done in this life for him either, and with that the forethought of our little Viola springs to life.

CHAPTER 4: STEEP HILLS

Frances took to brisk morning walks after a few months of returning home from the hospital, she loved the outdoors first thing in the morning because even the coldest winter day held promise, with the sun slowing rising like a best kept secret coming to light. Besides, she wanted to add strength to her bony figure and began the process of restoration from the years spent trying to bring Viola into the world. Most mornings she could be found challenging the somewhat steep terrain at the tip of the ravine with Maggie tethered to her waist and the handle of the pram tethered to her wrist. On this particular morning, attached to her tethered dependants, Frances was undeterred by the cold because she had bundled Viola from head to toe in what could best be described as a plush, weather resistant, mint green, hooded, zip up sleeping bag snowsuit contraption that resembled a papoose because it came with a matching green cap. Despite the cold Viola was warm and content staring up at the tree canopy soothed by the jostling pram and the occasional glimpse of her mother staring down at her.

The trio seemed not to exist at all from an aerial view, even from the ground they were barely visible through the thicket of trees, and one had to be in their immediate vicinity to even see them. They couldn't really be heard either and they walked as though they were alone in the universe, Viola in her rather soundless pram, Frances crunching the frozen ground beneath her boots, and the occasional rustling of leaves that interrupted Maggie's airy prance. The only evidence of their existence was the melody of clouds produced by their breathing that disappeared before they could even be detected by the birds chirping in the branches above. At the top of the incline Frances stopped and drew a breath, taking in the movement of the forest and feeling the glory of the morning. In what seemed like reciprocity for her admiration Frances noticed a blooming winter shrub with tiny pink flowers that appeared to be delicate but were actually resilient to the snow that had gathered over night. For some reason those flowers are Frances' last memory before the incident, as the event itself has vanished from her memory.

As she was considering taking a photo of the delicate snow flowers with her phone

Frances happened to notice a knot in the strap of the harness that kept Viola safely secured in the pram and she leaned into the stroller, unclasped the harness, and began to untangle the black rayon strap. This little gesture left Viola vulnerable at the worst possible moment for it was then that Maggie spotted a rabbit and in a move that was completely out of character she lurched after it with a force that in an instant pulled Frances flat on her back, knocking the wind out of her, which was a recoverable injury indeed were it not for the large rock that collided with the back of Frances' skull as her head hit the ground and she lost consciousness. When Frances hit the ground Maggie regained the sense of her prior obedience training and stopped what she was doing and licked Frances' face, looking down at her master with a look of confusion only available to dogs, and letting out a deep whimper in between.

In this impossible situation Maggie's actions would directly contradict her intentions, as often happens when we try to fix our mistakes or help the ones we love most. Maggie was smart enough to know that the people she loved beyond all measure needed help and not knowing how to offer it she paced back and forth between the

pram and Frances. All the jostling only
served to drag Frances a few feet and the
already frightful scenario took a turn for
the worse when with the force of Maggie's
pulling the stroller moved backwards
awkwardly. Then the momentum of the
incline took over and it started to roll
down the steep slope of the ravine until it
toppled over when it was interrupted by the
tether that was still attached to Frances'
unresponsive wrist as she lay unconscious.
Viola, who was no longer strapped safely
into the pram, rolled out of it, and like
a moss covered log in her slippery plush
green snowsuit, she slid downwards on her
back, unobstructed, as though a path had
been cleared for her, and like Alice down
the rabbit hole, she kept sliding until
she disappeared to the only pair of eyes
that bore witness to her vanishing, which
of course were Maggie's. Before I tell
you about what became of Frances after the
fall I will describe the journey of our
little Viola, so gather up the kids because
they will enjoy this tale of unfathomable
serendipity.

CHAPTER 5: THE GRECIAN CODE OF HONOUR

As you know the morning was cold and the ground frozen, so Viola, in the gaps between her fall, hydroplaned her way to the bottom of the hill and slid onto a flat patch of ice underneath an enormous old weeping willow, the very same willow that Frances could see from her front window, the one that she regarded as a mark of her place on the earth. The stretch of ice was so long beneath it that when her sliding plush green suit finally did make contact with the bark of the tree it made only a slight tap as if she were a curling rock with a pair of imaginary curlers sweeping the path ahead of her.

Startled by the single knock at the door Gilbert rose from his slumber curious about who had the gall to pay such an early unannounced visit. He threw his fine silk parlour coat over his matching silk pyjamas and looked out the peephole to an empty doorway. He thought perhaps it was Bunny's youngest playing a trick on him, so he opened the door slowly to take a look around and was moved by what he saw. On the bed of ice at the foot of his door was the largest green caterpillar Gilbert had ever seen, staring up at him with mesmerising dark eyes that looked as though they held teh mysteries of the universe.   Gilbert wondered why the caterpillar was making an appearance so early in the season, and why it had knocked at the door so early in the morning, and why it was on its back, but he dared not risk being rude by asking any of the questions. He remembered what he knew of caterpillars as they approached metamorphosis and thinking that his large friend needed a place of respite, he scooped up the caterpillar and brought it inside to rest and warm up.   He thought it wouldn't be too difficult to help this creature into its next stage of life and he had plenty of space for a cocoon in this large weeping willow he referred to as home.

Gilbert the III's kind heart was often overshadowed by his stoicism.   His large feline figure wore a tuxedo everywhere it went but Gilbert held such strong belief in decorum that he often covered up the tuxedo he was born with with fine clothes and was even known to wear real tuxedos from time to time as he would stand on ceremony whenever he had the chance.   He came from a long line of dignified cats and their gilded portraits hung regally on the large wooden walls of his home. Gilbert made light work of transporting his new friend into the kitchen and with the help of the arms from the head chair he propped the creature upright and placed a cutting board on the arms of the chair in front of its green puffy tummy. He then used a brown silk belt from one of his old parlour jackets to tie the cutting board to the arms of the chair. As he was fastening the knot to the chair with great precision he glimpsed into the eyes of his new companion and noticed something for the first time. He was mesmerised by the delicate features of its face and was taken aback because, quite frankly, he had never seen anything like it. As a matter of fact Gilbert found himself enchanted for a few moments when their eyes locked and he wanted nothing more than to continue to stare at this little face because it filled him with a joy he had never known. Although he didn't even realise it, he was purring contentedly, as he would do every time he met the gaze of those eyes from that moment forward. Right then and there Gilbert made a pledge to protect this beautiful creature and began to recite his family's traditional creed of honour without breaking his gaze:

"Through fields, and valleys, and all terrain
In service to you I shall remain
And when we part, we'll join again
All hail our Grecian honour"

Although there are six more stanzas to the Grecian family code of honour Gilbert stopped abruptly here because he was interrupted by a sound that shook him to his core. Much to his surprise the sound was coming from the caterpillar.

It was a piercing sound, like a kettle announcing its boiling point, and oddly enough it was also accompanied by water as Gilbert noticed a stream leaking from its eyes. The sound threw Gilbert into a panic, and he wanted to make it stop. He realised the possibility that the sound might have something to do with metamorphosis and remembering his creed he hoped that this wasn't the case. It then occurred to him that his friend might be hungry, and he put the kettle on for tea and began to put together a plate of something for the two to nosh on, but he had no idea what caterpillars ate and decided that freshly sprouted watercress might do nicely. As he hurriedly prepared the tea the shrill of the sound from the caterpillar bounced off the walls of the house and the regal frowns in the portraiture seemed to increase in disdain at the cantor.

Gilbert foresaw two problems that required immediate attention if he was to be able to feed his newfound friend with any measure of success. The first was the appendages that caterpillars usually have in abundance but were strangely missing from this one, which would make it difficult for his friend to eat. The second was having to abandon all decorum and stateliness that usually accompany a first time visit, which pained Gilbert because he loved propriety but could bear the sound no longer, so he set the table without a cloth and didn't make a trip to the hutch for the fine china. Once the food was out and the tea steeped Gilbert set himself to tackling the first problem and tried to assist his dependant with dining but was challenged by the wailing and the eye leakage. In his haste for silence Gilbert poured only a slight splash of hot tea into the bottom of the cup, added a spoonful of sugar, filled the rest up with milk, plunked a straw in and gave it a stir with a slight splash and raised the cup to the tiny mouth of the caterpillar.

Much to Gilbert's surprise the creature's lips sucked the straw and it swallowed a gulp of tea, and then another, as a peaceful silence was restored to the abode and the purring Gilbert marvelled at the expression of this friendly being enjoying what appeared to be its first ever taste of tea.   Just as the last sip was finished Gilbert thought that metamorphosis had begun because he noticed that right below the creature's neck the outer layer of green was starting to split and Gilbert wondered how this was possible without the formation of a cocoon when to his amazement a tiny hand poked through the split, followed by another tiny hand, and, locked in a stare with the deep brown eyes in front of him, for the first time, Gilbert realised that he was looking into the eyes of a human baby.

CHAPTER 6: FADING TO BLACK

Frances awoke to the face of a man she had never seen before staring down at her. He was on his cell phone reporting to the person on the other end that Frances had opened her eyes and there was a stroller but no baby. She had trouble making out his face but could see the trees above his head and cracks of sky peeking through behind him. In a gentle but commanding tone, he instructed her not to move, kneeling beside her as he did so. Moving had not yet occurred to her so this wouldn't be a problem. He informed his phone that they were about a kilometer up Make or Break trail, at the top of the incline. He then knelt beside her again and informed her that she had fallen, and that the ambulance was on its way.

Frances watched him as though he were a television program on in the other room, seeming to understand the gist of what was happening but not fully committed to the nuances of the show. Clearly, the meaning was going over her head. Just then she felt the warmth of Maggie's tongue over her nose, and she was attempting to touch Maggie's face when she winced with the pain in her head and put her arm back down. The pain was blinding now, and she couldn't hear or see beneath its weight, and she remembered Viola and a deep chasm opened inside her chest as she closed her eyes and mouthed a soundless "My baby" to the stranger before everything once again faded to black.

CHAPTER 7: LOLO
THE LITTLEST

While Gilbert usually succeeded at anything he put his mind to, he was for some reason unable to process why on earth he came to be in charge of a human infant, never mind the how, and he sat paralyzed until luck interjected, and he heard yet another knock on his door. As he answered the door Gilbert kept an eye on the infant, who seemed more contented by the tea. Gilbert opened the door to find Bunny's youngest, LoLo, who hopped in as usual without being asked. In her active way she managed to touch almost everything in the house within the first few moments of her arrival, chatting all the while with the details of her stream of consciousness as she did so. Her topics were vast and she asked Gilbert if he knew that today will have more sunlight than yesterday, but also that this is only true for half of the year. Without waiting for a response, she followed up with a non sequitur statement about the feel of the object she was currently touching (a silver thimble), and then she continued on about how more sun

and melting snow meant being able to go
exploring without being seen by Coyote.

She then mentioned that her mother
had seen Coyote's HUGE tracks close to
Gilbert's house this winter, the news of
which did cause Gilbert to pause pensively
for a moment.

At this point LoLo looked at the green
puffy entity sitting in the chair that had
somehow escaped her notice. She hopped up
on the table to get a closer look and in a
rare change of pace and tone she was still
and silent as she took in the other being
in the room and she released her grip on
the thimble letting it fall to the floor.
Forgetting about Coyote, Gilbert hastily
asked Lolo to look but not touch but LoLo
wasn't listening as she stared with her
mouth agape. Lolo watched in silence as
Gilbert, who had decided to help the baby
out of its pseudo cocoon, unzipped the
zipper of the snowsuit, took down the hood
and gingerly removed the green cap. To
their surprise, out popped a full head of
dark hair which appeared to be standing on
end. At the sight of the hair LoLo began
to laugh uncontrollably, and at the sight
of a tiny, tiny bunny laughing, Viola burst
into a full on baby cackle. So, like a
pair of giggling buddhas they revelled in
the mirth each had created for the other.

A palpable joy spread through the house and Gilbert found himself standing with no other purpose than to grin when for a third time that morning a knock could be heard at the door.

It was Bunny looking for LoLo. She entered in a tizzy, much like her daughter, but instead of the grace that accompanied LoLo's awe and wonder, Bunny bore the weight of worry and fret that life sometimes brings to mothers. She was muttering about LoLo's wandering away without permission when the scene at the kitchen table stopped her in her tracks. She demanded in a drawn out long whispery way to know what on earth we had here, as she slowly eyed the baby up and down. Without allowing time for a response, she continued to incredulously exclaim that this was indeed a human baby girl who looked to be very young indeed. Bunny had deep and vast knowledge of the humans up the hill, particularly babies, but how she came to possess it is a tale for another time.

She began to bombard no one in particular with one question after another, so quickly that it was assumed she was speaking rhetorically but nonetheless sought answers to where Gilbert had found her, where her mother was, whether or not Lolo was to blame for the situation, who was caring for this baby, had she eaten or had any milk, and was she warm enough. She then continued without delay to inform them that human babies wear something called a diaper and she asked if it had been changed and as sequiturless as her daughter she announced that someone must be looking for this baby and then she finally wound down her run on sentence when she looked into the baby's eyes and said something to the effect of how as she lives and breathes they are positively and then her voice finally fell silent as she fixated on the eyes that held the same magic as her little LoLo's did, and she felt the bliss of time stopping.

She continued in this state as she removed Viola from her snowsuit entirely and changed her cloth diaper with one she had fastened together with Gilbert's finest cotton tea towels, redressed her, and fed her a bowl of warm milk and soggy cookies with one of Gilbert's silver spoons. LoLo shadowed her mother and the trio were all smiles and little songs until Viola and LoLo played together on the carpet in front of the fire and both fell asleep mid play. In the meantime, Gilbert had prepared High Tea and he and Bunny sat at the table to talk about what was to be *done with the baby.*

CHAPTER 8: THE HUMANS UP THE HILL

Healing from the concussion was quick, painless and one might even say miraculous for Frances because the adrenaline coursing through her veins, pumped out by the need to find her daughter, dissolved any pain that she might have felt. Luckily the fall did not fracture her skull and although an MRI revealed a mild concussion, Frances felt no symptoms of her injury. As a matter of fact, she disregarded protocol and was back before dusk with the rest of the police team, neighbours and volunteers, searching for Viola. Fire crews had set up a rope that extended the entire depth of the slope and were able to rappel up and down the steep edge of the ravine without fear of falling. Only professional search and rescue staff had access to the rope and Frances watched intently as one figure after another climbed down to join in the search. The temperature was dropping by the hour and with the wind chill stung fingers and toes into numbness and although no one dared to say so near Frances, many had begun speculating that the cold had already claimed Viola.

Frances was impervious to this thought because she knew with every fibre of her being the certain truth that Viola was alive which only served to strengthen the urgency of locating her. Alban spent no time pondering his feelings but with a steady resolve he kept looking, and whether it was a testament to his confident stride or a gesture of pity, one of the rescue workers gave him a quick lesson on how to keep his balance while rappelling, and down the steep hill he went. The search was hampered by the full kilometre between where Viola fell and any place where a motorised vehicle could gain access, so although there was a semblance of an encampment for rescuers to warm up and volunteers pitched in and replenished hot beverages and sandwiches, the process was slow and laborious despite the many hands available to do the work.

Frances searched from the top and looking down she scoured every inch of the ravine for clues, for a bright green snowsuit, but because she was not allowed to climb down and get a closer look her efforts were futile and as the sun was parting for the evening there was still no trace of her baby daughter. Frances looked up at the silhouette of the massive weeping willow and in a moment of pause she implored it to protect her Viola with its majesty, as she did so she felt her late father's presence around her and she took a deep breath and could smell the sea he always brought with him, and she bade him to join the willow in guarding the granddaughter he had never met until she could be found.

CHAPTER 9: PREVENTING BLINDNESS

Now that we are thinking of Frances' father, I should tell you of the miracle that he worked in his life, for he had a heart of gold and an infectious smile, but it was his crippling pride that drew forth the miracle. He was born and raised on the shores of the North Atlantic Ocean and like most creatures he was so much a part of his habitat that he carried it with him wherever he went, but it was also so much a part of him that he could not see it unless someone pointed it out, which usually happened when they heard his accent. He had taken Frances to visit the place where he grew up when she was a little girl and together, they walked the hilly streets lined with the multi coloured aluminium siding row houses, at times against the ocean wind, but it was at their back when they finally made their way to the seashore.

Frances has such a clear picture of her father bending down and putting his hand in the ocean and then raising it to his lips to taste the sea and she remembers watching him as he celebrated his own private homecoming as if she were not even there. Looking back, she remembers feeling what he felt. He was a part of the ocean, he was a ripple that cascaded so far inland that he had lost his way, and his return to the vast unending waves reminded him that he was a part of something bigger, even if he was just a ripple because everything, after all, is nothing but the sum of its parts.

I know you must be wondering about the miracle but be patient, it is a slow-moving story and if you heard it all at once you simply wouldn't believe it. Hearing it this way, slowly, with every pointed detail, will leave you in such defence of its truth, that with a muted staunchness you will pass the tale to another imploring them to read it and see for themselves.

But let's stay where we are for now, with Frances as a little girl at the seaside watching her father bask in what created him. Frances' father was named Henry, but everyone called him Harry except for his mother to whom he would always be Henry. Henry's father was a pharmacist named George, by skill if not by credentials, for his understanding of how to combine various chemical properties in the quest to *cure what ails ya* (as he used to say) had become for him an artform. He learned what he knew from his employment with the local druggist, and the courses he took at university as he was planning on one day being a druggist himself.

Henry loved his father very much. When he was young, he would stand over his shoulder and read whatever his father was reading, even if it was a text about druggist training, just so that he could be around him. Sometimes he helped him with experiments, and he often did his father's calculations because his mind was so quick with mathematics that he could turn out an answer faster and more accurately than his father could, or at least that is what he was made to believe by his father.

Each day after school Henry waited for his father by the front window, reading whatever he could get his hands on while he did so. As time passed his after-school reads became longer and longer because his father began coming home later and later, usually staggering when he entered, and one June evening Henry found him sleeping on the front stoop. Henry had known the love of his father, as had his mother, but it was alcohol that won George over in the end. His compulsion to drink was so powerful that like a fruit fly to a glass of wine he followed the whiff of the drink, and although he knew it would kill him, he hadn't the power to prevent it, and he couldn't help but enjoy the buzz as he went down. He had dropped out of school and lost his job at the druggists and from then on Henry's mother Agnes had to work cleaning houses to put food on the table.

There came a point when those over the shoulder reads were nothing but a distant memory that Henry forever regarded as his last witness of his father's sobriety. Late one evening his father stumbled in as usual and in a terrible temper he began arguing with Henry's mother about the tin of beans he was expected to eat for dinner when he suddenly picked up the can and hit her in the head with it, gashing her head open with the jagged edge as he did so. That was the last night Henry spent in the same household with his father. Agnes recovered from the attack with a small visible scar on the right side of her forehead, but a gaping wound in her pride.

You see when she walked to the courthouse to file for a divorce from Henry's father, George followed her the entire way crying and pleading with her to reconsider, luckily Henry had been left at home and has no memory of this scene. Agnes was a proud woman and the shame of her husband's behaviour weighed her down as if she were tethered to an anvil. Indeed, because of it, she did not leave the house, for any other reason than to work or go to church, for two whole years.

She secluded herself from the squall of whispers circulating about how she should have dismissed the attack for what it was, a stupor of manly drunkenness, and for the sake of the family, she should let him stay. But Agnes knew in her core that if Henry lived in a house with his father he would grow up to be just like him, and she also knew that George would never want that to happen. She was strong enough to bare the scandal of a broken home and indeed, for the sake of her family, she made sure that he left.

Henry continued on going to school and from time to time he would see his father on the Central Street, swaying, and he learned to spot him from afar and change direction, but sometimes he would stop and talk to him and offer him what little money he had in his pocket. Henry claimed that his father's greatest achievement was his ability to produce strong, pure alcohol that could be consumed without the risk of blindness, but like all good deeds, the punishment was that he could see the demons he was facing everyday as clearly as he could see that he was powerless to defend himself against them.

I know we were to be getting to the miracle but again these things take time and I think it's best if we check on Frances before we hear any more about Henry, we left her with the smell of the sea searching for her daughter.

CHAPTER 10: SEARCHING

It had been a few days since Frances had fallen and the search party had thinned to less than a quarter of its original size. Most members of the party now referred to locating Viola as a recovery mission, so police mediators tried to prepare Frances for what they might find. Although she nodded at their rationality, she harboured the certainty that Viola was still alive and spent all day, every day, at the ravine. Alban too continued to search and although he was unable to hold the same certainty as his wife with regards to Viola's condition, he knew that it wasn't over yet and finding a resolution, finding Viola, was a mission that kept the horror of what he might discover at bay.

He had since shown Frances how to repel down the hill so she spent early mornings down the ravine and would climb up just prior to the search team's arrival. Maggie, who has aptly (given her role in the disappearance) and strangely (given her attachment to Frances) been absent from the narrative since Viola was last seen, was for the first-time accompanying Frances today. It was still dark as Frances repelled down the hill, and believe it or not, Maggie, who was so desperate to be of service that she was determined to follow Frances or die trying, scaled down the slope backwards with her harness tethered to the rope. Although Frances had scarcely slept since Viola's disappearance, she awoke from a brief slumber thinking that Maggie would be able to help, and watching her dog rappel down the hill gracefully affirmed that having Maggie with her was a good idea.

Frances headed to the foot of the large weeping willow, the place that for some reason she felt solace, and once there she sat on a log just under the lowest droop of the bare branch, so far from the trunk that it could hardly be believed that they were attached. She let Maggie off the leash because she was curious to see if she could sniff anything out. Dawn's rosy fingers were hidden by the pale grey sky as Frances sat, and, she wasn't sure how long she had been sitting in silence watching the dog sniff around before she heard something behind her. Maggie heard it too.

They turned to see a very large Coyote exposing its teeth as it glared at them, and from it came a low, threatening growl. Frances stood but was unable to shout at the creature before Maggie was ahead of her barking aggressively in the face of the wild dog. The coyote lunged forward at Maggie's neck but Maggie moved quickly and its large teeth dragged along the fleshy part of Maggie's hind leg. Frances had already picked up a stick and shouted as she attempted to scare off the animal with all of the aggressive force she could muster, which wasn't much, but Alban appeared magically behind her and the addition of his loud voice was enough to force a retreat from the coyote. Maggie continued to bark at the air that the coyote had left behind until Frances decided to take her back up the hill and tend to the rosy scratch on her hind leg, which, like a sepia portrait, was the only colour to be seen on this grey morning.

CHAPTER 11: BLUE JAY

The few days passed quickly for Gilbert as he was in a rather blissful state smitten with his new companion. He was currently engaged in one of his favourite activities which was feeding the baby mushed up biscuits and cream, although he did enjoyed everything he did with the baby, and he completed all tasks regarding her care exactly in the manner bunny had instructed him. As he did so he opened and closed his mouth awkwardly to the air, mimicking her actions and finding purpose in the twinkle in her eye as he did so. During feeding time Gilbert felt that each unified swallow, his imaginary, and hers of soggy milk drenched biscuit, was an epoch unto itself.

Suddenly, Gilbert was drawn back to the immediacy of the world by the sound of loud barking and growling outside the door, the former of which he seldom heard but the latter sound he recognized as Coyote's ferocity and so he hastened the baby into the bedroom fearing the hungry predator would sniff out the newest member of his household. Gilbert didn't know how long he was in the bedroom, or why he *even went to the bedroom, for Coyote had never given any indication that he was aware of Gilbert's existence. While he was there the baby had drifted off to sleep in the large basket that he had made into a bed for her, but which usually was purposed to contain linen.* The basket had a hinged lid that *Gilbert had* fastened to the bedpost to ensure that it would never close on the baby while she slept. When all was quiet Gilbert decided to go and look through the peephole and noticed his friend Blue Jay perched on a branch in the distance, so he propped open the door to say hello and inquire as to whether or not Blue Jay had seen Coyote. Upon seeing Gilbert, Blue Jay was as gracious as ever as he made his way over and watching his quick and purposeful glide through the air was almost as delightful for Gilbert as watching him perch between the buds of the closest branch, as if they had made room for him to do so.

After exchanging pleasantries Gilbert mentioned that he had heard Coyote earlier but also mentioned the barking and asked Blue Jay if he had heard or seen anything, to which Blue Jay replied in his usual expeditious fashion with an off topic remark on the increase in the number of helicopters he had seen recently and how they disrupted the tranquility of the area, and Gilbert steadfastly agreed (although he hadn't even noticed them so preoccupied with the baby was he). Then Blue Jay began to relay the account of the woman who was with the dog Gilbert had heard barking earlier. He had seen the woman daily in the early mornings as of late, but today was the first time he had seen the dog. For Blue Jay spent every dawn in the vicinity of Gilbert's home but moved on as the sun rose, which meant that he had always managed to miss the search party and was unaware of the team that traipsed through this particular territory each day in search of a green snowsuit. Gilbert, Bunny, and all of his usual visitors, also for some *unknown reason, had yet to catch a glimpse of the dramatic search and rescue efforts and knew nothing of the daily quest to locate the missing baby. Blue Jay continued to relay the tale of the Woman, the Dog, the Coyote and the Tree Branch in such alarming detail that none of Gilbert's senses were left un heightened by the velocity with which the tale was recounted. Just then Gilbert thought of the baby and although he knew she was safe in her basket he invited Blue Jay in for tea to continue the conversation so that he could be closer to her and shut* the door to keep the cold out. Blue Jay, who was usually reluctant to go indoors, thought it might be nice to enjoy a cup of tea for once and so he gratefully accepted the offer and Gilbert once again had the pleasure of watching him sweep through the door and into the kitchen where he took roost on the edge of the table as he had done in previous visits.

Gilbert had set the table for high tea as he did every morning after breakfast, and then again after lunch and dinner, lest he ever find himself unprepared to host an unexpected visitor, and he poured some tea into a thimble sized cup and set down an array of breadcrumbs and seeds for his companion. The pair had much to talk about and Gilbert began by filling Blue Jay in on the events that led to his current stewardship over a human baby, to which Blue Jay responded with a quick flutter to the bedroom to see the baby as she slept for himself, and returned before Gilbert could rise from his chair to accompany him. It didn't take long for Blue Jay to feel that they had exhausted the topic of the baby, which was a point unreachable for Gilbert, yet he could see that his guest did not share his enthusiasm for the finer points of infant care, and so he turned the conversation to what he knew to be Blue

Jay's favourite topic for beak wagging. He then made himself comfortable for the tale he knew he was about to hear, a tale he had heard before, and, a tale he rather enjoyed hearing his friend tell, and that was the tale of the Blue Jay, The Young Rabbit, and the Mouth of the Coyote.

Blue Jay began by recounting the details of the beautiful spring day three years ago when he was hopping from branch to branch, and he spotted Coyote prowling the earth below and decided to follow her just because he could. At first Coyote crept through the trees, head down, sniffing for a trail that led to sustenance, and every so often she would stand upright intently staring as though she had caught sight of something to prey upon and then continue when she realized it must have been a leaf blowing in the wind. Blue Jay followed Coyote for some time before he noticed something up ahead, something that Coyote had yet to see, and that something was Bunny's eldest PoPo, who busy munching on a large patch of wild sprouted watercress that had only just poked its head out of the earth.

Blue Jay had the omniscient vantage point of PoPo's impending doomful encounter, and knew he had to act fast to alert her in time to retreat because

Coyote was fast, much faster than PoPo, and he thought her only chance at survival was to avoid being seen. Blue Jay fluttered momentarily trying to figure out his best course of action, for he didn't want to reveal PoPo's position by drawing attention to the bunny as he flew in to warn her, but he soon realized that it didn't matter because Coyote was getting closer and closer and would soon see the little bunny regardless of how Blue Jay decided to act.

Sure enough Coyote spotted PoPo and bolted upright, her tail straightened and pointed downwards behind her and her back hunched, but wishing to remain undetected from the prey she was now stalking, she froze in an alert stance and then slowly started to creep forward with her head down. At that point Blue Jay flew as fast as he possibly could, and sang as loudly as he could until PoPo finally looked up from her munching and saw Coyote running towards her. PoPo instinctively began her retreat and her heart was pounding wildly because she knew she could not outrun Coyote, so she began scouring frantically for something to crawl into when she spotted a hollow log as she ran down towards the stream with Coyote swiftly approaching behind her. She knew she did

not have enough time to make it to the log
but she hopped as fast as her feet could
take her, stretching as far as she could
with each leap and expecting that her life
would end at any moment.

Coyote was just about to eviscerate
PoPo with his fangs when Blue Jay flew
in swiftly and in a rather awkward way
crashed into PoPo's right ear with his
long beautiful blue tail just as Coyote
closed his jaws and so the ear and the
tail were punctured simultaneously. This
last minute intruder startled Coyote, and
the blue flutter of feathers that she
chomped made her pause for just a moment
releasing her grip, which was enough for
PoPo to run into the log and Blue Jay to
alight on the nearest perch of a branch
above. Coyote was left standing outside
the log, so completely stunned by what
had just transpired that she gave up the
chase and continued on her hunt elsewhere.
So, the bird and the bunny had managed
to escape with identical wounds that would
eventually become scars on different parts
of their body, and to this day they both
agree that the ripping yarn describing how
they came to possess their disfigurements
was worth the fright of their life. As
a matter of fact, seeing them tell the
story together, which always ended with

lining up their respective identical holes left by Coyote's right fang, had become somewhat of a marvel at gatherings.

Just as Gilbert and Blue Jay were revelling in the excitement of the story and Blue Jay was showing Gilbert the small hole on his otherwise spectacular tail, a slight yawn could be heard from the baby in the other room as she roused from her slumber. This of course was Blue Jay's cue to depart, that and the fact that he had reached his limit for being indoors and was beginning to get antsy. So, he thanked his kind host and they exchanged a cordial farewell and Gilbert shut the door. He then eagerly headed into the bedroom to scoop up his favourite little tenant from her makeshift bassinet, with a deliberate refusal to let the thought of the eventual resolution of this situation with the baby, which he knew must come as night turns to day, spoil the moment.

CHAPTER 12: A POUND OF BUTTER

As she spent her days scouring the ravine for Viola, Frances occupied her time by continuing to beckon her late father's assistance and it could be said that even though he was not physically present, he was her constant companion in the way that Viola had been just a few short days ago. Indeed, the smell of the sea calmed Frances, and whenever she felt she was slipping into full blown panic she steadied herself with a deep inhale and the ocean's perfume hung in the air, as if it presented itself in secret for her detection only. Frances had always been fortified by thoughts of her father's strength, which might surprise you once you hear about Henry and his miracle ,so allow me to digress into that tale for a little bit.

Despite the trauma in Henry's household, his mother managed to stabilize their lives after George died, and they mourned the loss together. Somehow, Henry's father had been redeemed by his death, because from then on Henry and his mother exchanged stories of moments of the times when there was a third clever humour brightening the air in the home, and George's endearing presence could be felt in the house once again. Both Henry and his mother had acted as though he vanished on the night of the incident with the can of beans because from then on, the mention of his name became too painful to bear. Figuring that he was resting peacefully, they began to live with the memory of George as he once was, before the drink took him, and they let it fill them with the strength and resolve to move forward. Henry and his mother were easy companions until one day a tense moment of harshness shifted the trajectory of how Henry would eventually decide to raise Frances.

One Saturday morning Henry's mother had sent him to McGraw's general store on Central Street for a pound of butter and as he arrived, he noticed smoke billowing from the window of a three-storey house on the street where he was walking. Henry heard a woman calling from the third-floor window and she was beckoning as loudly as she could for anyone who could hear her to save her children.

Henry took a moment to assess the urgency of the situation and on the third shriek of *save the children* he ran over to the house and opened the front door and as the smoke thickened, he ran up the staircase in front of him. On the second floor he could see a little girl in one of the rooms to the left and he imagined that this was the child who needed saving, so he tried to scoop her up and head for the staircase, but she was having none of it, and flailed to get free all the while screaming for her sister.

Henry put her down, lowered himself to make eye contact and kept his calm as he asked about her sister's whereabouts, but the little girl had no idea where her younger sister could be found, and smoke was thickening by the second and the sound of the fire raging was deafening enough to drown out any screams for help that might otherwise have been heard. Henry felt the grace of God intervene, and something told him to sweep his hand under the bed in the other room and he did so immediately at which point he found the lost sister. All three managed to get back down the staircase to the front door only to realise it was shut and the doorknob was jammed. Henry put one child down and she clung to his leg for dear life and with the other still in his arms he prepared to kick open the door. Suddenly, the door opened on its own, and they made it out seconds before the beam above them collapsed with a fiery crash. Although they were all coughing and gasping for air, they were safe and sound, and Henry found himself standing in the cold of the exact same street, and in the exact same spot that his father had haunted when he was alive.

Looking up at the grey sky, he offered an obliging nod in gratitude for his safe keeping. To his dying day Henry swears that he heard a distinct click of the doorknob being unjammed and turning to open yet when they finally found themselves outside there not a soul was within ten feet of the inferno. He realised that the peril he had narrowly escaped could just as easily have come. After what felt like a long time talking to onlookers and explaining his story to the firemen who had just rescued the girl's mother, Henry finally headed back home without ever having purchased the butter he had come for.

In the meantime, Henry's mother had uncharacteristically worked herself into a frenzy with worry, for he had been gone for almost two hours on what should have been a ten-minute errand. She imagined that he had run into a friend, and he had gotten distracted and forgotten about the butter, but she knew he was not that inconsiderate and would never do such a thing without informing her, but then she told herself there was a first time for everything and so she went back and forth between worry and anger. She was in a rageful state as she had decided to put on her coat and go look for him, but he was approaching just as she opened the door and before he had the chance to explain what had happened, she gave him a swift cuff on the back left side of his head.

Henry was dumbfounded by the cuff, and his mother was shocked and horrified that she had done such a thing as indeed she now realised that there *was* a first time for everything. Her rage had disappeared with the energy of the clip round the ear she had given her son, so she composed herself, and embracing Henry she apologised, hustled him to the table, and then quickly put a cup of hot tea in front of him. After forgiving her, he began to recount the story of the sisters and the fire, and his mother was equally relieved that he was now safe, proud that he had been so brave, and mortified that she had greeted him as she did. Henry enjoyed telling the story and he went to great lengths to reassure his mother that the slap was nothing but a case of frazzled nerves until eventually they both basked in the excitement of the story. On that winter afternoon at the warmth of their kitchen table, Henry revealed the moment of divine intervention, and his nod of gratitude to his late father, and suddenly the pair felt like it had become a party of three.

In the moment of comfortable silence that followed the story Henry forged a plan to practice something that would protect him from the state his mother had been in when he came home. He decided then and there that he would always take ten deep breaths when he was overcome with any type of emotion, because for the first time in his life he realised that the potential power of the unchecked train of thought, in all of its sobriety, could have dreadful consequences in even the most rational and moderate being. He also knew that providence does not often show itself so clearly, with not only a door opening but a wake-up slap. He thought that if he ever had children, he would be sure to always follow the ten deep breath rule that had only just revealed itself to him, and thus was the shift in the trajectory of his life with the future daughter that he had yet to meet, and granddaughter that he would never meet, and the beginnings of a miracle in the making.

CHAPTER 13: SISTERS

Gilbert learned everything he knew about caring for the baby from Bunny, who had two daughters with whom you are already acquainted, PoPo the eldest and Lolo the littlest, and all three members of the Bunny family popped by daily to see the baby. But as the middle of the week approached, Bunny, out of a deep sense of maternal allegiance, exposed the feigned sense of normalcy about the current situation by wondering out loud who indeed must be missing this bundle of joy. Gilbert grimaced at the question and PoPo didn't seem to hear it, but for LoLo it was like a knife through the heart. It had never occurred to her before this moment that the baby had a family of her own. She imagined what life would be like for her mother if she were missing and the thought made her insides hurt with an ache that was different from any she had ever felt. From that moment forward the happiness of the time she spent with the baby, or thinking about the baby when she was not with the baby, was tinged with a long and deep sadness that seemed to be living in the air around her.

That night, as she and PoPo were snug in their beds, she began to think of ways to get the baby back to its mother. She imagined the baby's mother to be searching frantically, and weeping hollowly, which made Lolo cry into her pillow and she thought about talking to her sister about it, but then she remembered that PoPo never cries and she decided not to reveal her own tears. The funny thing about siblings who grow up in the same household, is that they are the only people in one's life who know and understand each other's lived experience, and LoLo and PoPo were bonded by this shared reality, but they were as different as two bunnies could possibly be. So, Lolo remained quiet but she knew that although her sister would not share in her tears, she shared the space in life where Lolo could simply be herself and know that she wasn't alone, even if she chose to keep her feelings to herself, and that was more than enough. In that comfort, she eventually drifted off to sleep with visions of a mother child reunion dancing in her head.

The next morning Lolo woke up early and hopped outside with two things on her mind, the first was what she knew she should absolutely not be doing, and the second was what she knew she absolutely had to do, and both as it happened were the exact same thing, and that thing was to go and investigate the humans up the hill. Now Lolo had a singular plan for this to happen and it wasn't complicated, for her intent was to simply climb up the hill and take a look around. She banked on finding a mother on her knees crying and imploring the weeping mom to follow her to Gilbert's willow. She knew not how she would accomplish the latter part of her task, but this wasn't enough to dissuade her from her plans as she resolved to cross that bridge when she got to it. So off she hopped towards the direction of the steep incline until she spotted a shrub filled with yummy buds and she couldn't resist munching a few before continuing on her journey. Now we must remember that there is nothing more vulnerable than a tiny munching bunny that is oblivious to their vulnerability, for even though Lolo must have heard the tale of the Blue Jay, The Young Rabbit, and the Mouth of the Coyote a thousand times, she still failed to see the similarity of her current undertaking with that of the watercress patch that began the adventures of her hole eared sister.

Naturally we will now discover that Coyote was indeed on the prowl but was still far enough away for Lolo to outrun her and she hadn't even spotted Lolo yet, so the situation was not yet dire. Lolo in the meantime was really enjoying the buds and she savoured each bite and as she crunched and swallowed slowly until she had had her fill, which didn't take much with her tummy being as tiny as it was. When she decided she had had enough and was to continue on her journey she hopped forward in the direction of the incline, and it was then that Coyote spotted her little tail as it bounced up and down with each spring in her step.

Bunny continued her contented prance, and as a matter of fact, she was so enjoying the beauty of the morning that she began to hum her favourite tune, Blackbird, as she traveled. This made it all the more difficult for her to hear Coyote, who had just broken into a full sprint after her, but unlike her sister, there would be no omniscient viewing Blue Jay appearing to warn her of her impending demise. Lolo had finally reached the bottom of the steep embankment and started to make her way up when she realized how difficult the climb was going to be. As she began her ascent, she started to make a game out of finding the tiniest ledges to balance her feet on and a path of little shelves with exactly enough room for her to hop appeared out of the hill before her and each step glowed as if the way had been lit by the fun of the game.

Still Coyote was almost upon her so it seemed as though this little game would be her last, for although she would reach the top of the hill, Coyote would get her as soon as she crossed the trail. The very same trail, known as Make or Break trail to humans, that Viola had strolled so many times in her pram before that fateful day that she toppled out of sight and disappeared. On went Lolo when she reached the top and the game now became trying to locate colour that had made its way above the white blanket of snow, so she hopped from the grey of rocks to the brown of branches and she even managed to step on some greenery that had been shed by a shrub, and she found enormous delight in the moment, only made possible because she knew nothing of her imminent role as Coyote's breakfast that morning.

But as luck would have it for Lolo, Coyote stopped in her tracks when she was a stride away from the top of the hill, for she had seen what Lolo had not, which was the search party of humans making their way down the trail. Coyote turned around once again, giving up the chase and and slowly making her way back down the hill.

As it turned out even Coyote knew better than to chance an encounter with the humans up the hill. As for Lolo, she merrily continued her journey and hopped away as if she were only waiting for this moment to arrive, without being noticed by or noticing the humans walking towards her, and never knowing how close she had been to the early end of being eaten.

CHAPTER 14: SALMON AND BREAD

There is a history behind everything we encounter that usually makes its way into the stories we tell, stories told in peaks and pitfalls that depend mostly on who is doing the talking. If we look at the history of Frances, for example, we find that she almost never came to be. As you know Frances' father was Henry, and his father a George, and before that a Henry and a George, and one more series of Henry and George before that, and then prior to that there was a Michael, who had a brother called Henry. Now Michael was an excellent fisherman because he never left the stream without salmon, and he was known for sometimes taking his catch to the local pub and offering it up so that all of the patrons could enjoy the splendour of fresh fish and ale.

He awaited the moment when they would in unison raise their glasses to Michael in gratitude for the provisions, at which point he would bashfully bask in the gesture of his own generosity. Michael so enjoyed the revelry that from the moment he awoke he imagined the catches that would be for the purpose of the evening's festivities and set off to make it happen. One Saturday morning, after he set his net in the stream, he sat with his Irish wolfhound Conan, and imagined how the evening crowd would enjoy his catch, failing to notice the freshwater pearl mussel on the creek bed below him.

This particular mussel happened to be 134 years old, it had been around the George that sat on the edge of the stream before this Michael and the Henry before that George. It had been present for everything from christenings to drownings and managed to survive the famines and the plagues suffered by the humans above it in the peace and tranquillity of its underwater home. It simply existed, emitting the silent vibration of its being, and although it had gone undetected it somehow carried with it the history of its ever-changing environment, offering little wise pulses, which was the only thing it could really do.

Lost in his thoughts and stroking Conan's wiry fur, Michael began to think about Molly, who was the reason he was catching the fish in the first place. He hoped to marry Molly and he often saw her at the pub enjoying his salmon, but had only once had the courage to go over and talk to her, at which point she coughed up a fish bone and he walked away feeling guilty for having been the cause of discomfort to her delicate throat. Despite the round of cheers for the salmon, he left the pub that night in poor spirits.

As it happened Molly was interested in Michael as well, but he couldn't see this fact through the veil of his own self-loathing, and he imagined his affection to be unrequited. As he was thinking about ways to approach Molly he looked into the stream, and wouldn't you know it he finally noticed that there lay a freshwater pearl mussel within arm's reach. He scooped up the mussel out of the water and pried it open with his small knife, killing it instantly, not realising that he was erasing 134 years of pure calm energy that had only moments ago been permeating the water beneath him. Much to Michael's delight inside the mussel he found a beautiful shiny pearl that he knew would help to make Molly his wife.

Molly stayed home from the pub that evening with a headache, and Michael wasn't bothered by her absence because he was so delighted with finding the pearl that he celebrated and drank more than he could handle, and he awoke the next morning in one of the beds at the local brothel, having no memory of what brought him there. It was the only time in his life that Michael had done such a thing, but it was also how he made his way into an early medical text called, *Venereal Diseases The Uses and Abuses of Mercury in Their Treatment*, which was commissioned by the vice-president of the Royal College of Surgeons in Ireland and published in 1825.

The case of poor Michael can be found in Chapter 31. As it happened Michael had contracted a venereal disease and was so overcome with the effects of the illness that he suffered the loss of half of his reproductive organ. But as luck would have it for him, he was cured by a mixture of poultice and mercury, with only a few minor setbacks until he was discharged from the hospital, *perfectly well* according to the account in the textbook. That he should overcome such a plight is a testament to human resilience, but that he subsequently should start a family is nothing less than providence. As it turned out Molly decided she would marry him anyway, and she didn't care about his one and only visit to the brothel because she thought of the future they would have together rather than the past the had spent apart. They eventually married and lived as married couples do, Molly wore the pearl around her neck but was known to claim that she would have married him with or without it, because she loved him so strongly. Despite Michael's intimate injury, he did his part in bringing his son George into the world, and George in turn would eventually have a hand in the production of a Henry, who would have a George, who would have a Henry, and then one more George and Henry would lead to the existence of Frances and of course our little Viola.

As it turned out life triumphed and generations flowed, but of course this story might read a little differently if it were written by the pearl oyster. But seeing as we do not have that particular story, we will have to rely on the version in which we are currently immersed. I will suggest however, that if you ever come across it, you consume the tale told by the immortal jellyfish (Turritopsis dohrnii, according to scientists, but Morty to his friends). Morty is the only living creature we know to be immortal, and Morty was a close friend of our ill-fated freshwater pearl oyster, a friendship forged when they met in passing and the two formed an instant connection. Morty's version of the events leading to the demise of our dear and beloved friend the pearl oyster are quite different than the one you are reading, and if you are ever lucky enough to acquaint yourself with that particular version, I suggest you relish every word. For now, however, we have no choice but to continue with this one.

CHAPTER 15: GILBERT'S WILLOW AND THE MAN WITH THE AXE

Perhaps we should also examine Gilbert's lineage. Gilbert came by the place he called home honestly, for Gilbert's mother had made her home in this very willow, as her mother had made hers, and her mother's mother hers, and so on we could trace this willow back for at least three centuries of the Grecian feline clan. And that is how it came to pass that one of the most magnificent trees for miles around became known as Gilbert's willow. That being said it was never actually believed that the willow belonged to Gilbert, for who could claim title of such a thing of majesty, because every knotted twist of the intricate detail of its labyrinthian trunk, and the eternal grace of each willowy branch, were so clearly ordained to be as it was, as it is, a marvel to behold, and not a possession to be owned.

Gilbert was therefore ever grateful for being able to reside where he did and had no inclination that the willow belonged

to him, rather he lived in perpetual
gratitude to the tree for allowing him to
reside there in the nestle of its heart
and said so out loud each night before he
slept, just as he had been taught to do
by his ancestors. Plus, Gilbert was not
the only creature to reside in the tree,
for many a living thing sought respite
in it, and so from its branches to its
leaves, to its bark, to its roots, it was
the consummate host of living entities,
which meant that this glorious willow had
experienced lifetimes upon lifetimes upon
lifetimes of splendour as it stood rooted
in unwavering being.

It is hard to believe that it had been
a century and a half since the man with
the axe rose at dawn on the shore of Lake
Ontario and walked north for most of the
day until he spotted the tip of the willow
and thought it was as good a place as
any to camp for the night. Horizons can
be deceiving though, and he hadn't counted
on the steep embankment he would have to
descend, nor had he realised how difficult
it would be to find the tree in the thick
of the woods, but he reoriented himself
continuously by looking up for the sway of
the tallest foliage, until find the tree
he did.

He wasn't even sure what compelled him

towards the tree, only that since he had seen the top of it from a distant dirt track that he was travelling for no reason in particular, he felt beckoned by the billowy branches dancing in the breeze of the summer day, as if they were asking him to come see the tree up close for himself. When he finally arrived he lay down beneath its branches and from under the canopy he could see the light of the late afternoon sun streaming through the leaves as they took their place among the symphony of clouds that drifted in the vastness of the sky and made it seem like anything was possible.

He lay there for a long time watching the play above him unfold without even realising that he was doing so until he saw something with his peripheral vision and sat up. He froze when he realised that a black bear was between the trees about thirty feet away. He had known his walk ran the risk of bear sightings and was prepared to frighten off the bear with a small jar of coins that he had slowly just retrieved from his bag. He shook the coins in the jar as loud as he could, and the bear, startled from the sound, ran up the closest tree. So now he knew he had to create some distance between himself and the bear and also that he had to keep an eye on the bear as he walked away from it, which would be difficult to do in the thick of the forest, but necessary because his retreat might prompt the bear to charge. As he began to formulate his next move, he retrieved his axe and gripped it tightly as he started walking backwards and for the first time he noticed a small greenish glow in between two raised roots of the tree. It was so small that it had almost escaped his detection, but it seemed to slightly increase in size as he stared at it, and he thought that maybe it was moving.

Then he thought maybe he was looking at a firefly, but the green of the glow rid him of this belief. He stood perplexed under the canopy of the willow, staring down, axe in hand, with the bear looming in the nearby tree like a memento mori in this living portrait. The vignette conveyed the very piece of work humans are, for in his infinite faculty and noble reason, this paragon of animals was so transfixed by the growth of a phosphorescent mushroom expanding before his very eyes and revealing the glory of the force of life all around us, that he remained still in the moment because he recognized that the force of life that pushed up the mushroom is also in ourselves.

If the tableau had been painted by an

artist it would certainly hang in the most prestigious art museum in all the world, maybe it would have been called Man with Axe (circa 1888) and been an impressionist piece with the colour of the mushroom so true to life that it would be impossible to replicate, and it would only ever exist in this painting. But we don't need it to exist in that way now because it has a rather more fitting place in the art gallery of your mind.

The man eventually made his way backward and continued on his journey, but for the rest of his life on the planet he felt the life force of the phosphorescent mushroom in himself, until he left the planet and continued to feel it in a way that I couldn't recount even if I tried. I sure can feel what he felt when he saw the mushroom though. I hope you can feel it too, and if not, maybe take a seat beside Gilbert's Willow, who has been embodying it for centuries, and if you can't find Gilbert's Willow, any old willow, or tree for that matter, will do nicely.

CHAPTER 16: COYOTE

Gilbert was purring away as he fed Viola when Bunny knocked on his door for the second time that day in search of LoLo. It was mid morning and Bunny had been searching since she realised that LoLo had snuck out but was unable to find her. She sat herself down at Gilbert's table with an imploring look on her face, the likes of which Gilbert had never seen on Bunny and in this state of intensity Bunny began to share her thoughts. Coyote liked to eat. It is not so much that she liked to eat as that she had a burning in her belly for food that always had her searching for something to ease the burn, but of course the fix was always temporary and like Sisyphus' boulder, the burn always remained.

This meant that anything that Coyote might eat should always have their guard up, and if there was one thing that Bunny knew for certain, it was that LoLo never had her guard up, not for one moment of her life, for she didn't even really understand what that meant. Once, Bunny had seen LoLo balance on one foot on the top ledge of the back a kitchen chair,

reaching as far as she could with a sharp
all steel butcher knife, in an attempt to
get toast out of a plugged in toaster, and
she didn't even scold her, she just put
her arms around her and lifted her down
onto the seat of the chair, and served
her toast and tea at the table. She then
talked of LoLo laughing with a mouth full
of soggy tea drenched toast at something
funny PoPo had said, completely oblivious
to the peril she had just escaped, and it
sounded as if it were one of the happiest
moments that life has to offer on the heels
of what could have been a tragedy.

The reason that Bunny was now telling
this to Gilbert was that she knew that
if she did not find LoLo she may never
find LoLo because there would be nothing
left to find.   For LoLo could not keep
out of harm's way if she didn't even know
that harm had a way to be kept out of.
After he finished wiping the baby's hands
and face with a warm damp cloth, Gilbert
suggested that they ask Blue Jay if head
seen anything, and they opened the door to
find PoPo approaching with a worried look
that revealed before she had to even say so
that she had not found her sister.   Blue
Jay was nowhere to be seen so they went
back into Gilbert's living room so that
PoPo could warm up. Bunny's expression had

not changed, and it did not take long for them to formulate a plan. Gilbert would keep an eye out for Blue Jay and Bunny and PoPo would continue to circulate the area between home and Gilbert's for any sign of LoLo.

Gilbert watched mother and daughter hop away in their respective directions and then he canvassed the air and the branches above for Blue Jay and seeing no trace of him, he headed inside to sit at the front window and wait for Blue Jay to appear. He had just out the baby down for her morning nap and in the silence he began to worry about LoLo.

Bunny was as determined to find LoLo and after leaving Gilbert's willow she made her way to each of LoLo's favourite places until she noticed a path, but not really a path as it was completely overgrown, but she decided to follow it anyway because she just had to look wherever her thoughts lead her to look. As she made her way through the foliage thickened and she felt that even if LoLo were in here it would be difficult to see her. She decided to turn around and go back the way she had come when she spotted a hollowed out old tree trunk with a gaping hole in the front that was overgrown with various kinds of shrubbery, and she went over to take a look inside the hole.

She was beyond surprised to find a nest of four Coyote pups sleeping and cuddled together so closely that it was difficult to tell where one began and the other ended. As soon as she saw the pups, she knew that Coyote was bound to return shortly and that she was most certainly searching for sustenance, so she quickly made her way out of the thicket to avoid becoming lunch. As she hopped away, she thought of Coyote nurturing those sweet little pups, licking them clean and offering them milk, and she wondered how it could ever be so that creatures had to feed on each other's young. She tried to make sense of the impossible notion that one young life had to be sacrificed to save another, and how unfathomable it seemed to her that the magical presence of her little LoLo should cease to exist so that those soft and delicate pups could thrive. But she also winced at the thought of harm befalling the new little siblings asleep in each other's comfort.

In this horrible conundrum Bunny began to make her way to Gilbert's Willow once again, to find Blue Jay, to hear about what Blue Jay had seen, for he must have seen something and have something to report about the location of her little

LoLo, if only because she couldn't bear it if he didn't. As she continued her thoughts once again drifted to the pups and the burden of hunger and she rode this thought all the way into a vast future where hunger didn't exist. Maybe physiologies would morph, and sustenance would be ethereal, so that no being need eat or drink or relieve yourself at all, because the dance of life was recognized by all who drifted in and out of it and the beauty of being was the only purpose of taking any shape at all. She began to consider that she had overthought her encounter with the pups because of the stress of her missing daughter when she finally approached Gilbert's Willow once again and discovered Blue Jay gracefully perched out front, indeed in possession of a tale of her daughter's undertakings this very morning.

CHAPTER 17: FRANCES AND THE STURDY IRON RAKE

Dawn's rosy fingers had departed, and the sky had lost its pink and turned to pale orange when for the second time that morning Frances left her house and began to make her way to the ravine. It had been almost a week since she had seen the eyes of her Viola in real life, but it seemed that they were always with her because she could think of nothing else but the soft and delicate features of her baby. She spent her time warding off the bleak terror of nothingness that life offered without Viola by staying outdoors as much as she possibly could. The neighbourhood kids still came close to pet Maggie sometimes, but Frances became so preoccupied with locating her baby and she hadn't the time nor inclination for pleasantries.

Once though, a six year old girl from across the street that had been calling on Maggie for what seemed like always, and had loved Viola as dearly as her tender heart could, stopped Frances and threw her arms around her waist. She hugged Frances tightly and begged her to bring back Viola adding that she knew she would find her, tears streaming as she muttered sentiments that would have been indecipherable to one who was not in that exact situation at that exact moment, but Frances understood her completely and she let her own tears flow, hugging the child back as if she were catching the magic of youth and faith through the exchange. A flock of geese flew above their heads as the embrace ended and they slowly parted company, and it seemed as though the geese had grabbed the release of emotion and flew away with it. For Frances continued on her way and the little girl headed home, but both felt fortified by the purge that was now making its way to a patch of grass on the wings of the gaggle.

Since the fall, Frances slept rather fitfully on the couch in the front room by the window so that whenever she opened her eyes, she could see the silhouette of weeping willow behind the houses across the street and implore it to keep Viola safe until she could find her, so deep was her connection with the willow that it was the only thing that could lull her into a couple of hours of tormented sleep.

Alban slept on the couch across from her and eventually he rearranged the furniture in the room and pushed the couches together

so that he could be near her. He felt
that as long as some part of his body was
touching hers and he could feel that she
was asleep, he too could fall into a brief
and afflicted slumber. Every morning he
would put the furniture back in its place
as if he didn't want the disarray of the
room to reveal the slow unravel of their
life. His job had become finding Viola
and he spent his days methodically combing
through the area where she fell, sometimes
in the company of others and sometimes
on his own, but always knowing that he
must have missed something and holding
a rational belief that she was still alive
because there would certainly be evidence
both to and of the contrary, and since he
had found neither, he continued looking.
In the far reaches of his mind there was
a little idea brewing that someone might
have found her and been keeping her, but it
was pushed down as soon as it popped up by
the notion that two such horrors could not
possibly befall one little family.

Maggie had already been for a walk that
morning and Frances left her at home as she
sometimes did, but she would come back and
retrieve her later in the afternoon, and
once again in the evening, when they would
head to the ravine. She zipped up her coat
as she walked down her driveway and stopped

in her tracks when she saw a baby bunny, so tiny it could fit in the palm of her hand, hop towards her from in between two houses across the street. It hadn't seen her, and it was hopping and stopping, and hopping and stopping, repeatedly and Frances stood watching the dainty creature, and she found herself a little in awe because she had never seen a bunny that was so puny, or so cute. After standing still for a few moments on the sidewalk, the bunny started hopping quickly towards Frances again, and this time it didn't stop. This time it headed in a straight line across the street until it fell between the sewer grate and disappeared from view at the bottom of Frances' driveway.

Frances looked in the sewer to find the bunny splashing in the frigid water as it tried to recover from the three foot plunge, but there was no perch to climb on the cold, concrete, underground wall. Horrified, Frances looked up to see the neighbour from across the street, who had seen the whole thing, running towards her.

Together they instinctively lifted the heavy sewer grate and Frances thought to retrieve something that would lift the bunny from the garage and so she ran and pressed the automatic door opener and ducked under as soon as there was an

opening tall enough and came back with
a sturdy iron rake. Frances leaned down
into the sewer as far as she could and
she scooped up the bunny as if she were
collecting spaghetti from a pot of water.
The bunny was barely moving now and its
breath was shallow and almost non existent
when Frances finally got her hands on it.
She held it against her and she hurried
through her front door on a quest to tend
to the dire condition of the frozen baby
rabbit.

When she entered the house, she grabbed
two terrycloth bibs from the diaper bag
that was on the deacon's bench at the
front door, dried the bunny off with the
first, and used the second to swaddle the
creature. Then she sat on the couch in
the front room, laid it on her chest, put
her coat over it, and finally took a deep
breath as she felt the breathing of the
bunny quicken and she knew that it was
still alive. She looked out the window
and found such solace in the weeping willow
watching them as each breath of the bunny
strengthened her certainty that her Viola,
like the small bunny recovering on her
chest, was also still alive.

Frances wasn't sure how long she sat
breathing with the bunny but eventually
it woke from its slumber and raised its

head. It sat up and froze when it noticed Maggie. Frances had already commanded Maggie to sit which was unnecessary because, since the fall, Maggie's only purpose was to serve Frances, and so she spent most of her time sitting close to Frances, at the ready. Maggie had seen the entire thing take place from the front window and her instinctual predatory nature with rabbits had been replaced by the need to mend what she had broken, and though she knew not how, she was ever attentive to the who, which was of course Frances, and so the bunny was what Frances dictated it to be.

Frances held the bunny and carried it with her until she found something comfortable enough to make a home for it, which as it turned out was a beautiful soft cloth lined wicker hamper with a hinged lid that had been a shower gift from Grover and was currently empty in Viola's room. So, Frances placed the bunny in the basket, closed the lid and went to find water and food for the little creature. Maggie followed the pair around until all was settled and the baby bunny was cozy in her hamper home in Viola's room and Frances decided that she must get to the ravine. She instructed Maggie to look after the bunny as she zipped up her coat and headed *out the door in search of her Viola.*

CHAPTER 18: LOLO, MAGGIE, LAMBY BUM AND THE BROKEN NECK

LoLo had been hopping joyfully, still immersed in her game of locating colour when she realized that she was no longer in the forest and was in the land of the humans up the hill without ever realizing how she got there. She was not afraid of getting lost because all she had to do was look up for the branches of Gilbert's willow and she knew if she hopped towards it, she could make her way back home. She stopped and used her peripheral vision to take in the strangeness of so much concrete and felt a little pang at the thought of the grass and trees that must have been here before it. She noticed a seagull flying above, a squirrel on a nearby roof and trees both large and small scattered around and she breathed a sigh of relief that nature had adapted somehow to the humans up the hill for now. She was also grateful for the steep ravine because she could never imagine the lot of living entities that she encountered daily finding any space up here.

LoLo noticed a woman across the street and for some reason she couldn't explain, she was drawn towards her and so she began hopping excitedly to get noticed and beckon the woman to follow her back to Gilbert's willow, and that was the last thing she remembered before finding herself here in this basket, which she couldn't help but notice was quite dark despite all of the light that made its way in through the wicker. Thus was the tale that LoLo had recounted to Maggie who was currently lying in the hallway and listening to the story while keeping an eye on her as Frances had requested.

Maggie hadn't really responded to LoLo as yet, for she really didn't know what to make of the tiniest bunny she had ever seen, and she wasn't one to befriend critters when she normally felt an innate obligation to keep them off the property, or at least alert Alban or Frances to their whereabouts. This was the first time Maggie had been able to chat, or should I say listen to a rabbit, for the conversation was very much one sided until finally at some point LoLo drew a breath and asked for Maggie once again to open the lid of the hamper for a bit so that she could see the brightness of day in its proper form.

Maggie responded by stating that Frances had wanted to be sure that the bunny would be secure and not get lost in the crevices of the house and that no matter what she would always abide by Frances' wishes, especially since Viola had dissappeared. Maggie even had a mantra that she repeated more often than she cared to admit, and it almost seemed as though she ended every sentence with it as she resisted LoLo's persistent queries about letting in some light and in a low, slow and soft voice Maggie declared that _for the love of Frances_, the absolute safest place for her was the soft, comfortable and warm hamper she was in, and that it would be best if she could just grow accustomed to her new surroundings.

LoLo really was persistent though, and a hint of panic crept into her voice and Maggie began to think that Frances would not want to see the poor little creature suffer with claustrophobia, so she began to discuss the possibility of opening the lid to the hamper if LoLo agreed to stay put. LoLo unequivocally agreed that she would stay in the hamper if Maggie were kind enough to open the lid. So, Maggie used her powerful snout to nudge the hamper open and she poked her head inside and opened the soft close hinge lifting the lid of the hamper until it was upright.

Maggie and LoLo stared at each other for quite some time, and each had the exact opposing thought of their counterpart so to save time I will start with Maggie and move to LoLo and as I describe the polarity of their perspectives, it can be assumed that whatever one is thinking the other holds the exact opposite view. For starters Maggie marveled at LoLo's diminutive stature, and LoLo was astounded by the rather dank smell of the breath that showered over her, while Maggie was struck by the precision with which LoLo's tiny feet climbed the delicate ledge of the wicker hamper, leaving LoLo to wonder about the length of Maggie's never ending fur as she propped her front paws up on the hamper still towering over LoLo and on went the repelling stream of thoughts between the pair until Maggie sat on the floor, and LoLo on the edge of the hamper making them as close as they were going to get to being eye to eye. Unless of course we consider the possibility of LoLo leaving the hamper.

Once LoLo was able to size up Maggie, she drew a deep breath of appreciation to the sunshine that was shining on her face through the window. She closed her eyes to really feel the warmth of the sun and then

opened them and began to look around the
room. She had never before seen anything
like what she was seeing. She so admired
the beauty of this space that it was lucky
she drew a breath because she held hers
while she took in what she saw around
her in this delicate room on this bright
sunny winter day. I should tell you that
Frances and Alban had commissioned an art
student at OCAD who lived up the street
with her parents, to paint a mural that
replicated as many of the works of Beatrix
Potter as she could on the wall in Viola's
nursery. The walls were therefore adorned
with the most beautiful paintings that
LoLo had ever seen, and they weren't even
in frames, they were just painted directly
on the wall. The delight of seeing them
take up space altogether on the wall was
best personified by LoLo's pleasant facial
expression, and watching LoLo admire the
art on the walls was a sight that belonged
on the wall she was admiring.

The portraits on the wall consisted of
a rabbit in a blue coat holding up a sign
letting us know that his name was Peter,
and there was a cat in a beautiful pink
dress washing her kitten's face with a
sponge and the help of a dainty wash basin,
then there was a mouse with a top hat,
a squirrel with a nut, and a cat pawing

away at a tea cup. There were many more
delicate little creatures looking magical
in various little scenarios and underneath
all of them the name Beatrix Potter could
be seen, scrawled in tiny writing though
it was. LoLo had always been told she
was clever and she could read the writing
on the wall that told her that she was in
the room of someone named Beatrix Potter.
LoLo began to imagine what the occupant of
this room, this beautiful Beatrix, must be
like, for the most charming room that was
ever to be seen must certainly house the
most exquisite creature in all the world,
and at that she asked Maggie if she could
locate Beatrix.

Maggie had no idea what LoLo was talking
about and she was about to respond as such
when LoLo bounced from the edge of the
hamper to the base of a nearby dresser to
investigate something else that had caught
her eye. Maggie reminded LoLo that she
was to stay in the hamper beginning her
sentence with <u>for the love of Frances</u> as
she liked to do but LoLo was too interested
in what she had found to pay any attention
to Maggie. LoLo was sitting on the dresser
now, staring into the tiny eyes of a bunny,
the likes of which she had never seen
before. It had very, very shiny skin
and it was brownish but was wearing a blue

coat like Peter on the wall, and it had two of the most beautiful glossy little ears on the top of its head, and his shininess was just so perfect and striking that LoLo could hardly refrain from letting Peter know what she thought. Indeed, LoLo loved the ears of her new friend so much, for they were so delicate and beautifully shaped she decided it would be the first thing she would say to the wonderful Peter but was a little uncomfortable when she received no response.

Maggie watched with amusement as LoLo tried to communicate with the Peter rabbit figurine that had been Frances' as a child and let LoLo in on the idea of porcelain ceramics, breaking it to her that the creature was inanimate, it wasn't really alive and that the conversation with him would therefore be a little one sided. LoLo was amazed, and a little frightened by the idea and she reached out to touch it, just to see what it felt like when she saw something behind it that made her heart race and she hopped towards it as quick as she could and the slight tap of her foot knocked Peter rabbit over which for some reason was enough to break the neck of the delicate figurine, and sever the head from the body. LoLo wasn't the least concerned about the crash because she was standing in front of a framed picture of the baby, it was in black and white and the baby was propped up on the shoulder of her mother, so all that could be seen was the mother's long hair flowing down her back while the face of the baby was clear as can be with her eyes as delightful as ever. LoLo realized that she was in the baby's room, the baby that they had all come to love, the baby that was currently residing in the Gilbert's willow, that baby, LoLo realized with joy, was Beatrix Potter!

As LoLo stared at the picture a silence washed over the room and Maggie couldn't find the words to even begin talking about Viola, and LoLo's eyes were torn away from the picture by Maggie's palpable sadness, at which point LoLo realized how much Maggie must be missing Beatrix and she could hardly contain her excitement when she blurted that she knew where the Beatrix was and could bring Maggie to her right now! Hearing this Maggie stared at LoLo, a little dumbfounded, wondering why she called Viola by the name of Beatrix, until she understood that LoLo was saying that she could find Viola and didn't care what she called her. Maggie then muttered <u>for the love of Frances </u>and not knowing what else to do, she put her front paws on the dresser in a standing position, and, as

LoLo filled her in on the details of the baby and her little nest with Gilbert, she began to lick LoLo's face. LoLo laughed at the comedy of how gross it was to be licked and their shared exhilaration at the joy of the imminent mother child reunion was as deep and flagrant as it was brief. For Maggie could contain her urgency no longer and she decisively coaxed LoLo back into the hamper and sat on guard like she had been instructed, waiting for Frances to return, empowered, and invigorated with the knowledge that now was the time to bring back Viola.

Frances returned before the sun had set and she immediately went upstairs to find Maggie on guard in front of the nursery and LoLo in the hamper sitting contentedly. She went over to the crib and picked up the beautiful little soft stuffed lamb that she had called Lamby Bum when she used it to play peek a boo with Viola. She thought of touching the lamb's soft face to Viola's nose and the glory of her baby's crooked smile washed over her. Thinking of Viola's smile, she opened the lid to the hamper and placed Lamby Bum in the hamper with the tiny bunny as though the gesture somehow comforted her own daughter. Frances closed the lid and headed downstairs asking Maggie if she wanted to go for a walk as she did so, never having noticed the broken neck of Peter rabbit, which both LoLo and Maggie had forgotten all about.

CHAPTER 19: RISE ABOVE IT, EVEN IF I CAN'T

Frances had buried her father when she was seven months pregnant and being all too familiar with loss, she never afforded herself the luxury of real grief lest it permeate to Viola who was comfortably housed in her womb at the time. So as Frances searched for Viola, she also felt her father's presence. She began to connect with her father's memory, and she could feel very strongly that he was with her while she searched. She thought of herself as a little girl and remembered when she fell off a swing and had the wind knocked out of her, it was her father who knelt beside her and coaxed the breath back into her body by having her slowly count to ten and breathe deeply as she did so. Henry watched his daughter struggle for breath and kept his calm knowing that the only way for her to regain steady oxygen was to watch someone lead by example. From then on Frances heeded the ten deep breath rule whenever she injured herself but it wasn't until she had her heart broken for the first time that Henry taught her how to really heal herself, for ten deep breaths coupled with the mantra he taught her, could ease even the deepest pain. She was a teenager when she had argued with some friends who had joined in excluding her from play for no other reason than they could, and she returned home crestfallen and in tears to be greeted by her father.

Seeing her in this state he sat beside her and he said that she must always rise above it. He said to imagine that she was crying because they had thrown a hot coal at her, and then told her that she wouldn't be hurt if she didn't catch the coal, and even if she caught it and it stung for a bit, she need only breathe deeply and let it go. In the end, Henry said, you are the only one who can be accountable for what you do and think, so always treat unkindness with kindness, because unkindness in another is nothing but lack, and engaging in lack will only beget lack. Then he said that if she was able to rise above it, she would take others with her, and without her even realizing it, Frances had found the purpose of her life.

Frances thought of another time when she was walking home one fall day with the wind blowing her hair, and she felt something extraordinary. She felt something within herself that lifted her and filled her with connection to everything she was seeing, and the connection was so deep that she began to lose herself in the peace of the walk. She made her way home and started running when she saw her father raking the leaves on their front lawn and as always, he dropped what he was doing when she arrived. They played on the front lawn for a while and the clouds blew in and it looked as though it was about to rain and in the distance a lightening shower lit up the sky and together, they revelled in the light show, which proved that life had more to offer than the ruse of everyday purported it did.

Henry had decided to study mathematics, well it was more of a calling than a decision. He had won mathematics competitions in every grade of school until he reached university and after winning both the campus mathematics and chess tournaments his mathematics professor recommended that he attempt the Mensa IQ test, which indeed led to a membership into the prestigious and exclusive club of geniuses. Henry never did rest on the laurels of his intellect because his wife, Pearl, did that for him. Pearl was a good mother to Frances and made her feel special and loved her unconditionally.

Armed with his credentials and accolades Henry climbed to the most senior position in a private corporation, purchased some land and built a mansion for his family without ever realising that he too had lost himself while he wasn't paying attention. For he had begun to identify with his prestige and when things fell apart, markets crashed, recessions began, positions dissolved and the house had to be sold, his inner strength disappeared and rising above it no longer became an option for him.

Henry was never able to own the breakdown he suffered when he lost everything, and his pride crushed every chance he had to regain his sense of self. He played solitaire until he developed dementia. Alzheimer's made away with his autumn years and by the time he died, the he that had been Henry who knew that he was a part of something bigger was long lost to him, although it was still there hiding behind the shame. Pearl stuck by him, still boasting his Mensa IQ to anyone who would believe it. Frances would sometimes be called to collect him, like when he once ran out into traffic and got hit by a car because he was scared and confused so he just started running. Aside from a bruised arm and the plaque that was slowly destroying his brain he was fine when she got to the ER, as always overjoyed to see her.

Frances remembered the time she picked him up from his day program because her mother had tried to steal two hours to get her hair done. He was unable to understand that he was at Frances' house and that Pearl would be there soon. He grew so agitated that she eventually put him in the car and drove around in a snowstorm. If they were in the car, it meant we were on the way to Pearl and he was as comfortable as he could be in the perpetual wait, like most humans he was either focussed on the past or the future, failing to see the moment he was actually in.

Eventually Henry was placed in a long-term care facility where he attacked a caregiver. Frances did not see her father in the months before his death, and she tries not to picture him diapered and restrained, which is how he spent his final days.

Frances had learned to rise above it from her father, even though he couldn't do so himself, and this was the miracle he had done in his life. He had taught someone to do what he was unable to do. She was strengthened whenever she felt his life force. She could also feel the Henry's and the George's that came before her and even those that would come after her because like the moment of the light show, she saw the vastness of life that she, Viola and everyone else for that matter were blessed enough to embody, and she knew that this vastness was here to be felt no matter who or what managed to be able to give it a home. Frances also knew that once she saw vastness of life as she did, she would never be able to unsee it, and this vision was the single greatest achievement of her life. As she searched for her Viola she was fortified by his words, and she knew she would rise above it because she was miraculously steadfast in her belief in miracles, which, incidentally, is the only requirement necessary for them to happen.

CHAPTER 20: THE WARMTH OF THE FREEZER

Frances and Maggie headed back to through *Make or Break* trail as the sun was setting, but neither noticed the glory of what seemed like a painting above them in the sky as each second held the magnificence of living and breathing on earth right there in full view for all to embrace if only they knew enough to choose to do so. Missing it entirely though, as they thought of Viola, they carried on through the trail, Maggie dreaming of the imminent reunion and Frances still holding the memory of Lamby Bum. Together they made another round of the usual area until they located Alban and the other search and rescue members who were just beginning to pack up for the day.

As the twilight dwindled Alban watched Frances and Maggie walk towards him and his heart jumped at the sight of her as it always did, only lately he also felt her pain too, and relieving it was as much of a driving force for him as finding his daughter safe and sound. He thought of the darkness that would soon be upon them and realized how big a part it played in making the fading sun glow, and on this sixth night of separation from Viola the sight of Frances in the distance was different somehow, and he knew that this chapter would end soon, and that their remaining chapters as a family in this life would be left in its afterglow, be what it may. But the feeling of having this moment, this very moment, as he drank in the vision of her silhouette, and relished the mere fact that Viola even happened to be born and alive on the planet, was strangely enough for him. He felt in some way they were all together right now and that they always would be at the same delta, a place he knew not how to describe with words, but if I was asked, I might call red Jell-O. He could feel the life force that was keeping them alive, all of them, and he knew that no matter what happened, the sense he had in this very moment would forever be available to him and that all he had to do to feel it was to pause and let it be.

He walked to greet her, and they embraced instinctually and as tightly as they could with their winter coats, and he somehow transferred his recent intimation to her through the warm hug, or perhaps it had been she to him from the relief of the bunny rescue, or maybe it was Maggie's confidence of knowing all would be well because the LoLo tiny bunny would lead the way to Viola. Whichever way it came to them, they all felt a little lighter as they made their way home with Maggie strolling beside them, once again in possession of her usual transcendence.

When they arrived home, they went upstairs to the nursery and Frances showed Alban the little bunny and then retrieved her breast pump and sat in the rocking recliner to pump some milk as she had been doing since she last saw Viola. Frances was determined to keep her supply up for when she was once again reunited with her daughter. Alban cleaned the poop out of the hamper and refreshed the bunny's water and food and then lay on the floor in the nursery at the foot of the rocker holding the bunny on his chest as he listened to the mechanical pump drone away as it worked to fill the bottle with expressed milk. Frances had done a little research and was advised to return the bunny to the ravine so they decided that tomorrow would be the day to bid farewell to their little guest and that they would bring the bunny with them in the morning when they headed back to the search area, without even noticing Maggie and LoLo exchange and excited glance when they heard the plan.

They left the nursery when Frances was done with her pumping and she placed the warm bag of milk in the freezer with the other bags that had accumulated as evidence that there was indeed a baby for whom the generous supply was intended, and Frances admired the stockpile in the freezer for a moment because she knew it was the best way to keep the milk warm and flowing. They then ate peanut butter and jam sandwiches and settled themselves on the couch in the front room and Frances searched up the best places in the forest to return a bunny to the wild and if I didn't know better, I would say that the pair was beginning to feel as if Viola had already returned. For some reason the gloom and dread that had filled the house lately were slowly escaping like the smoke from a chimney. Once Frances and Alban had fallen asleep Maggie made her way up to the nursery and talked with LoLo about how they would reunite the family and after formulating a solid plan, they bid each other good night and adieu and Maggie once again licked LoLo's face a few times as they wished for each other's safe keeping. The house then quieted as Maggie fell asleep on the front door mat and LoLo curled up as cozy as could be with Lamby Bum and also drifted off to slumber.

CHAPTER 21: THE FRETTED HOUR

Bunny hung on Blue Jay's every word as he explained what he saw happen to her little LoLo and the party moved inside Gilbert's Willow as they listened. Gilbert was purring ever so softly as he carefully and happily watched the baby chew on a large shiny spoon that she clutched in one hand as she sat in a makeshift contraption comprised of pillows, silk ties, and a step stool and yet was somehow as safe as any infant seat the baby had ever graced with her presence. To hear Blue Jay speak when he was excited was a marvel in and of itself, but to hear him recount the tale of LoLo, The Sewer and The Humans up The Hill, as it would come to be known ever after, and for the very first time at that, was almost too riveting for Bunny to bear. PoPo had since knocked and was just in time to hear it from the beginning.

Blue Jay told it rather quickly and then delivered the unexpected news of humans coming down the hill and into the ravine, which sometimes happened but never

in the way that Blue Jay described, and
this prompted an unfamiliar expression of
distress on Gilbert's face. For Blue Jay
noted that the group of humans (one of
whom was responsible for LoLo's rescue)
were clearly in search of something that
they hadn't found yet. He knew this because
this was the third day he had seen them
and he had adjusted his usual daily flight
pattern so that he could keep an eye on
their undertakings, because he knew that
the unpredictability of human behaviour
had the potential to make every dweller in
the ravine uncomfortable.

Blue Jay continued to note humans
should be avoided because their habits
were so incongruous that one could hardly
imagine that what could be said of one
could be said of another. Humans, he
said, had a capacity for cruelty not
only towards animals and nature, but also
towards each other that far surpassed any
creature known to the natural world, and
it was a well known fact that some of them
would kill for sport and not sustenance,
and that some were capable of torture for
amusement, while others were known for
benevolence beyond all measure. Blue Jay
learned everything he knew about humans
from Owl, who had learned what he knew from
his grandmother. Owl's grandmother said

the best way to understand humans is to know that there are two types, and she had come to know this through her vast stint residing at the library clock tower while reading over distant shoulders through windows which allowed her to both sharpen her eyesight and occupy her time.

So Blue Jay reiterated what he knew of humans according to Owl's grandmother as follows: first, he said, there are those humans that are full of sound and fury as they strut and fret the hour upon the stage that is their life, which then becomes just a tale told by an idiot, signifying nothing, until it is heard no more. Second, there are those that know that there is nothing either good or bad, but thinking makes it so, and they reside in virtue that exists within all humans when they can rise above mere thought, and these humans live out their days in service of this virtue until they dissolve back into it, pointing the way for others as they do so because they understand that the fretted hour of the first type of human is but a blindfold that the second type of human has been blessed to remove.

Bunny and Gilbert were a little lost at this point, but they agreed that humans poking around elicited a general air of discomfort to all who lived in the area.

This was best conveyed through Gilbert's face, with his furrowed brow frozen in thought, for he had an inkling that the humans poking had something to do with the baby, who currently sat on her makeshift throne, still marveling at the spoon in her little hand. Bunny hadn't noticed Gilbert's face because she was preoccupied with LoLo's current circumstance and although she felt a little better knowing that LoLo was alive, (which she hadn't doubted for even a second) and that she was in the possession of a human woman who saved her from drowning and was probably the second sort of human, she still wanted her LoLo back with her and began to focus on how to make that happen.

Gilbert in the meantime, had begun to purr softly as he stared at the baby, but what he had known since he first discovered the baby began to percolate, which was that no matter how much he loved her, she must go back where she came from even if he knew that to say goodbye to her would surely break his heart.

After saying all that he had come to say Blue Jay excused himself and both Bunny and Gilbert watched him fly away between the branches in the sunlight of high noon, and the vision left them full of promise as it always did. They decided to first forge a plan to get LoLo home, and then to buck up so that they could do the same for the baby. Bunny, as I have mentioned, was acquainted with the humans up the hill (yet the time for that tale is not now) and she had planned with Blue Jay to be shown the house where LoLo was living tomorrow after breakfast, and while that was happening Gilbert would place the baby in the path of the humans who were sure to return.

For even he agreed that getting the baby outdoors for the first trek of the search party in the morning at dawn would be the best way to get her home. Mostly because it was as soon as possible and he thought the quickest departure for the baby would be the most painless, like ripping off a Band Aid. The sun was setting by the time they had laid their plans for the next day, and they indulged in high tea prepared and served by Gilbert while Bunny and PoPo enjoyed being around the baby. Then, thinking of the early morning tasks, Bunny and PoPo decided that they would go home for the evening, and left hastily knowing that there would be time to say goodbye to the baby in the morning. Gilbert was purring softly as he always did when he was with the baby but at the moment, she had only just discovered her right foot and he was sharing in her fascination with the *appendage, so he stayed where he was and nodded politely, asking Bunny to shut the door as they departed.*

CHAPTER 22: THE QUIET OF THE MORNING

Bunny and PoPo left Gilbert's willow resolute in their plan to be reunited with LoLo but as they started to walk home her absence hit them like a tidal wave and they trudged on knowing that they would arrive to find their home emptier than the walk that carried them there. They made the decision to pretend that LoLo was already home but sleeping in her room and they didn't even open the door lest they wake the invisible sleeper and interrupt their make believe world, in which neither were very content but each for the sake of the other pretended enough to get through the night. They woke before dawn and at daybreak they made their way to Gilbert's willow to find him just having finished setting the table for high tea and waiting for the baby to wake up. He had laundered all of her belongings, including the makeshift ones that he had sewn together and the snowsuit, but he knew that she would leave in the same outfit that she wore when she arrived and that everything else would be left behind as a reminder of his time with her.

They enjoyed the sparsity of conversation in the quiet of the morning together as they were all focussed on missing someone, either impending or present, and because their respective thoughts generated the same energy, they all found themselves in good company. After they had eaten Gilbert began to prepare the baby's breakfast and Bunny insisted on occupying herself with the dishes from the high tea, ignoring Gilbert's vehement protests that she leave the mess for him to clean and the kitchen was spotless and the breakfast ready in no time, when right on cue a yawn could be heard, and Gilbert changed her and placed her in the makeshift high chair, and took a moment to admire her cute morning face. All three of them enjoyed getting the baby ready this morning and PoPo had become quite good at getting a smile from her and rather than think of the series of lasts that were happening, they all just stayed pleasant as Viola ate and had her hands and face washed and she was dressed in the clothes she had come in and was ready to meet the day.

The sun was starting to rise now, and they all knew it was time to start looking for Blue Jay, who was to warn them of the approaching search party so that the baby could be placed in their path. Sure enough, just as Gilbert had the baby all bundled up, they could see Blue Jay approach through the window, and they made their way outside and watched him as he fluttered his wings briefly and eloquently just before perching on a nearby log to inform them that the party had started making its way down the trail towards the incline. At this Bunny and PoPo said farewell to the baby for they were going to the foot of the incline to size up the humans who were in possession of little LoLo. Although their goodbye was quick it wasn't as painless as they had anticipated and as they hopped away both were tear filled and heavy hearted at the thought of the baby's departure, for they really had come to love her, and their sadness increased because they knew that LoLo would miss the chance to say goodbye.

Blue Jay flew back to the trail to keep an eye on the humans as they had discussed. He left without really saying much of a goodbye to the baby, but before he bid farewell to Gilbert he did make eye contact with him to tell him that he had always admired the strength of his feline friend because he knew that sometimes doing the right thing is the hardest task of all but that he was honoured to have a friend like Gilbert, who was a living reminder that difficult tasks can indeed be done. Gilbert stayed silent but nodded and then watched Blue Jay fly away, and in the pink of the early morning he admired the grace of his friend's silhouette before turning his attention to the baby.

CHAPTER 23: LOLO'S RETURN

Frances and Alban rose early as usual that morning and Frances expressed some breast milk as Alban tried to find something they could use to pack up and carry the bunny back to the ravine. They had a quick coffee as the day was breaking and by the time the sun began to rise, they made their way to the place where they usually joined the other members of the search and rescue team. The team was surprised to see the bunny in the cardboard box and agreed that the foot of the incline was probably the best place to let the little creature free. They walked together, Alban holding the box with the bunny and Frances holding Maggie's leash with their right hands, and clasping their warm gloved left hands on the inside as they continued walking along Make or Break trail.

The morning was quiet and there wasn't much chatter as they approached the top of the incline and as dawn appeared, her fingers bright, they reached the bottom of the hill and started looking for a place to let the bunny go before they continued to search for Viola. Frances walked towards an old Blue Spruce that had a lovely warm spot about two feet high below the base of its first branches and it seemed like the perfect place to leave the bunny so Frances put the box down on its side and opened it so that the bunny could simply hop out, and hop out it did, and as quickly as they had come to know the little creature, they watched with both relief and sadness as it hopped away to find its way in the world. When it hopped out of sight the team began walking their usual path and Maggie stared at the space the bunny had left behind for a moment before joining the group in their walking. They decided to split up and a team of search and rescue operators headed one way while Frances and Alban headed towards the large willow and for some reason, despite Viola's absence, the air held a hint of promise.

CHAPTER 24: THE COLD PINK NOSE

LoLo hopped as fast as she possibly could towards Gilbert's willow the moment she was let go, until she ran right past her mother and PoPo, who were calling her from behind a tree, and she finally stopped. It took some time because she had been moving with such force that she needed a moment to turn around and hop towards them. But hop she did, and the trio reunited with such enthusiasm that they were simultaneously knocked down and held up by each other's embrace. It wasn't long before LoLo blurted out that she knew who the baby belonged to, and Bunny and PoPo filled her in on the plan to return the baby to the search party as they all hopped quickly towards Gilbert's willow. LoLo looked forward to being able to tell Gilbert that the baby's name was Beatrix Potter, and she recited the formal introduction she would make when she presented Beatrix Potter to Gilbert III, as she raced to make it in time. She pictured the joy on Gilbert's face that would come when he heard her name for the first time and the delight that was always found in the eyes of the baby.

★

Gilbert had just made his way to the spot they had all agreed was best and he laid the baby in the snow not far from the willow and she looked up at him and smiled at the vastness of the sky and the branches above him before focussing once more on his face. He purred gently and knew that now was the time for him to take his leave and hide behind a nearby tree and watch as she was scooped up by the arms of her mother and he had to say goodbye once and for all. He snuggled his cold pink nose on her little warm face one last time and although he wanted to pledge the Grecian code of honour, he couldn't get the words out because the heaviness in his chest was crushing him and he told her he loved her, and swallowed hard, and tears flowed as he walked away silently and hid behind the closest tree.

★

Frances, Alban and Maggie walked towards the willow in silence. Frances noticed a beautiful Blue Jay flying above them as they walked, and she paused for a moment to watch it fly past them and its silhouette looked so remarkable in the pink of the morning light that she nudged Alban to point it out and they both watched the graceful bird until it flew out of view.   As they continued walking a butterfly flew out in front of them. It appeared to come out of thin air.   In disbelief, all three of them watched it, wondering how on earth it had come to be flying around in the winter and where it would go with no perch left uncovered by the dusting of snow that had fallen overnight.   Well, at least that is what Frances and Alban were wondering.   Maggie wanted to chase it, but was held back by thoughts of seeing Viola and was on the lookout for the little bunny who had promised to come back and lead the way. The butterfly flew away disappearing back into the air somehow and turning the hint of promise they were all feeling into a bit of magic. They walked on a little further as the sun cast a light that made the splendour of the forest visible, and, just as Frances and Alban saw the willow in the distance, they spotted the unmistakable shade of bright green that they both immediately recognized as the plush warm snowsuit, and they started to run.

★

From behind the tree Gilbert was hoping

that the humans up the hill wouldn't take too long to find the baby because although the snowsuit was warm, the cold, snow covered ground would make sure that it didn't stay that way for long. At that moment Gilbert saw something moving quickly through the trees and as it approached, he realized in horror that it was Coyote who had begun to charge towards the unattended baby. Without hesitation Gilbert also ran towards the baby to defend her, and just as Coyote was about to close its teeth on the baby's face Gilbert pounced and Coyote's powerful jaws closed in on his neck. Not expecting the mouth full of fur, Coyote released and let Gilbert drop to the snow beside the baby when she noticed some humans and a dog running towards her, and rather than risk an encounter with humans, she ran off in search of something else to feed on. At that moment Frances, Alban and Maggie approached Viola and the cat lying in the snow, not noticing that Bunny, PoPo and LoLo had arrived just behind them, and Blue Jay had also arrived above them.

Frances dropped to her knees, scooped up Viola and wept as she held the skin of her baby's face to her own and Alban had his arms around both of them as she did so, and his shoulders were heaving with the open weeping that consumed him as he held his family in his arms once again. In this weepy, shocked, and confused state they looked at the cat that had just saved the life of their daughter lying in the snow and noticed that it was still alive. Frances stroked its head as she realized that the poor creature had been badly injured while saving her daughter's life, and not letting go of Viola she stretched down beside it and kissed its furry face, and, in doing so, accidentally grazed Gilbert's cold pink nose with Viola's cheek. A gentle purr could be heard from him as his blood spilled onto the snow and the life that was in him departed, molecule by molecule, until the purring slowly subsided and Gilbert died right there with everyone he loved while he lived gathered around him. Frances noticed that Viola was looking at the cat as though she were familiar with him, only because she knew exactly what face her baby made when discovering something new, and this wasn't it. Viola stared as if he were still alive, not knowing the difference I suppose, but she cackled and laughed into the air around them amused by something that only she could see, and the distinct smell of the sea wafted through the air.

Maggie allowed herself one lick of

Viola's face which seemed to break everyone out of the trance they had been in, and Alban decided they ought to get Viola to some warmth. Together the family exited the ravine, and Maggie looked back to see the bunnies, that neither Alban nor Frances had even noticed, surround the cat and she felt a pang of sadness for her littlest friend LoLo, for although she was reunited with her mother, she had lost her dearest friend. Maggie knew of Gilbert, if only through the love that seeped from LoLo's description of how he cared for Viola. Maggie could see what LoLo could not, that Gilbert's care for Viola reflected his pledge to care for LoLo herself, so innocuous that LoLo hadn't considered that the Grecian Code of Honour (in its entirety) had been pledged to her long ago, when she was too young to have any memory of the event. Maggie understood from remembering LoLo's words the deep loss of the moment she was glancing back to witness. Even though Maggie had never met Gilbert, she knew he left a hole in the universe that could only be filled by the story of how he spent his days while he was here, the story currently being intercepted by you. The story that at this moment brings Bunny, PoPo, LoLo and Blue Jay to their proverbial knees in agonizing *grief.*

★

Many nights and days passed before Bunny, PoPo, LoLo and Blue Jay even began to adjust to life without Gilbert. They buried their friend as close to the willow as possible and they hung the most beautiful portrait of him on the wall at the head of the table beside the painting he had done of Beatrix Potter (thanks to LoLo they now knew her name) so that they would always be present when high tea was being served by Gilbert's daughter, who returned to the willow from her brief residence with the humans up the hill after hearing about the death of her father, but that of course, is a tale for another time.

EPIOLOGUE

Viola continued to grow with Frances, Alban and Maggie watching her series of firsts in life (teeth, steps, words) together with delight to be a part of all of them, knowing how close they had come to losing her. Frances often thought of the miracle of the cat in the snow that died saving her baby. She thought of the day that Viola's stroller tipped, and she watched in horror as her baby slid down the hill. Frances and Maggie followed as quickly as they could right behind Viola. Frances had been horrified when she caught sight of the coyote running towards Viola as she was scrambling to get down the hill. She couldn't believe her eyes when the cat appeared out of nowhere and the coyote attacked the cat instead, simply because it had interrupted the trajectory of its charge toward Viola. Maggie's barking and Frances' shouting were enough to scare the coyote away and Frances scooped Viola up and examined her to see if she were injured on the cold winter morning. Viola was unscathed from the fall and had not a scratch on her because she was protected by her snowsuit, but Frances realized that if it weren't for the cat the coyote would probably have attacked Viola. Frances bent down to comfort the cat, which was a tuxedo cat with a pink nose, handsome and regal looking, even in death Frances thought. She pet the soft fur of the creature and stroked its cold pink nose. She was shocked to discover that it was purring while it died, and she wept in both sadness and gratitude beside the dead creature. When she thinks of the day that she watched the cat die, she shudders at the image of the blood-soaked snow, knowing that the blood could just as easily have been her daughter's.

This memory always grips Frances with immense and deep fear, and when she is overcome by it, she pauses and takes ten deep breaths. On one sunny afternoon, after quelling a fearful episode Frances feels a strong urge to do something to honour the beautiful cat, whose presence had been so fleeting in her life. So, she sits down with her pen, and an empty black writing book, takes ten more deep breaths, and, writes a sentence about remembering being born...

OUR LIFE IN RED JELL-O

Seeking To Bolster Mental Health For Families On The Heels Of The Pandemic, Kerry Greco Wrote A Novel As A Master's Thesis On Mindfulness In Education. Our Life In Red Jell-O Takes Us On A Journey Inward To Solve The Mysteries Of The Universe By Looking To Your Own Heart. Read It Alone, Or With Children, And Discover The Strength Of Who You Are.

Manufactured by Amazon.ca
Bolton, ON

32292125R00079